Precious

Gems

For Your Mind

*Wisdom, Tips, and Quotes for
Experiencing an Amazing Life*

Well Done Life
Series

Also by Chris Warnky

Heart of a Ninja Series

The Heart of a Ninja: Stretch Your Boundaries

What Just Happened?: The Line

What Just Happened?: The Run

The Heart of a Ninja for Kids: It's Play Time!

Twelve Traits of a Ninja: Live Like a Ninja

Four Traits of a Ninja: Experience the Ninja Fun

Well Done Life Series

How to Refocus Your Life: See beyond the Urgent to the Big Picture through Personal Retreats

Turning Gray: A Spiritual Shift – Leading to Greater Awe of God and Creation

The Coach Approach: A Unique and Supportive Way to Give and Get Help

Precious

Gems

For Your Mind

Wisdom, Tips, and Quotes for Experiencing an Amazing Life

Chris Warnky

Well Done Life LLC
Columbus, Ohio
2024

CHRIS WARNKY

Well Done Life

Copyright © 2024 by **Chris Warnky**

Library of Congress Control Number: 2024909974

Ebook ISBN: 979-8-3302-9251-6
Paperback ISBN: 979-8-3302-9250-9
Hardback ISBN: 979-8-3302-9253-0

All rights reserved. No part of this publication may be reproduced, distributed, or transmitted in any form or by any means, including photocopying, recording, or other electronic or mechanical methods, without the prior written permission of the publisher, except in the case of brief quotations embodied in critical reviews and certain other noncommercial uses permitted by copyright law. For permission requests, write to the publisher, addressed "Attention: Permissions Coordinator," at the address below.

Chris Warnky/Well Done Life LLC
1440 Mentor Drive
Westerville, Ohio 43081

Dedication

I dedicate *Gems* to my nieces, Delaney and Sarah, who recently graduated from college, and to my nephew, Dalton, who I had the opportunity to visit with during a trip in 2023, and to my other nephews, David and Jonathan, and to my three grandchildren, Hannah, Lydia, and Grace. Also, for those who at times, have voiced frustration to me about where they are in life and how life seems to be going.

I dearly want to provide all of you with love, support, help, and some concepts, tips, and tools to help you enjoy your life even more. The concepts in *Gems* can and will change your life, and your many years ahead, making them greater than you ever imagined by planting these concepts in your mind, meditating on them, then making wise choices and applying them on a daily basis.

Contents

Introduction 1

The Value of These Gems 9

Chapter 1: Big Picture 12

Chapter 2: Spirituality 16

Chapter 3: Feelings 19

Chapter 4: Thinking 22

Chapter 5: Adversity 39

Chapter 6: Priorities 41

Chapter 7: Planning 46

Chapter 8: Doing 56

Chapter 9: Personal Growth 71

Chapter 10: Relationships 79

Chapter 11: Employment 94

Chapter 12: Money 97

Conclusion 112

More about Well Done Life Services 114

Acknowledgments 115

About the Author 116

Introduction

How often do you wonder what you should do in a situation or wish you knew more about a topic so you could make a better llife decision or feel reactive to life, feeling like things keep happening to you more than you would like, or wish you could be more proactive, more in control of your real-world experiences? If you can relate to any of these situations, then help is on the way. A different form of education is literally in your hands, education that is focused on how to better live and experience life in your day-to-day world.

What if you could go to college and get a bachelor's degree, a master's degree, and maybe even a doctorate for free? It wouldn't cost you hardly any money, time, or effort to get that education, and you wouldn't even have to learn the lessons the hard way, through making mistakes. Wouldn't that be amazing? That's exactly what I hope *Gems* will do for you, provide you with practical knowledge and wisdom, an education about how to live this life well without having to spend the money, and four to eight years in school to learn it. How to daily live isn't taught much in schools. In *Gems,* I share over 150 life concepts and quotes that I've learned during my sixty-seven-plus years of life. Most are quite short and simple, but they can make a tremendous impact on enhancing your life experience and future. I hope they do, and I hope you're attracted to these ideas and concepts and that you're continually drawn back to them, over and over, just like they've done for me, molding me and shaping me into the person I am today.

I wish I had had a resource like this when I was younger. I could have eliminated many mistakes that, to some degree, have limited my success and health. I'm quite thankful for all I have at this age, and it could have been even easier and better had I known these things much earlier in life. I hope this is a tremendous benefit to you at a much earlier age.

You might already have your high school diploma and maybe even your college degree, or more, but reading and applying these concepts will be like getting your degree, your education, and your university credentials, not for study in a particular field, but for living life.

I've Been So Blessed

I've lived a blessed life and have been retired now for over 11 years. This has occurred due to God's provision and blessing, a tremendous number of repeated wise choices, and the learning and insights I've gained from my personal experiences, as well as what I've learned from others from their experiences. Writing and publishing *Gems* is a way to share many of the factors that have influenced me and had a tremendous impact on my life. I hope that many others can also be positively influenced by these ideas that can dramatically help improve life.

I get so pumped each time I come up with another way to make a positive impact on others by improving their thinking, which can lead to an even better life for them. I dream of providing them with a broader perspective, new ideas, and deeper thoughts than they've ever had, with an ability to see longer range than they previously have, to better understand the impacts of their thinking and actions, so they experience many fewer surprises and achieve many of the things that they truly desire. I hope *Gems* is another way to make a difference in this world, to create an even greater legacy, hopefully making an impact in a positive way on many others.

How Gems started

The idea for writing *Gems* came during a drive to and from Arkansas from Ohio. I was looking forward to visiting with family members during some key family events that were occurring on the upcoming weekend, including a funeral home visitation for my sister-in-law's mother, who had recently passed away within the week. The next day, my niece, Delaney, was going to be graduating from Arkansas on Saturday night. And Mother's Day was that Sunday. It had been years since all three of Mom's kids had been together with her on Mother's Day. It was going to be a special day.

During the drive, I was reflecting on life relative to the loss of a loved one, the major accomplishment of college graduation, and the celebration of a mom who had raised three kids who were now in their 60s. It made me think about my life and the many things I've learned and would have loved to have learned even earlier in life. As I thought about what I've learned by age 67, it occurred to me that I could pass some, or maybe even many of them down to others younger than me if I simply documented them and provided a short description of how they've positively influenced my life. My first thought was to convey the content and insights by producing short YouTube videos. My idea was to produce one and share it each week, revealing many of the things that have shaped and changed my life. Someday, I might still do that.

As I started to list my key thoughts, which kept coming and coming to mind, I began to think also in terms of publishing another book that could be a quick read for family members and others, a reference that hopefully could be thought-provoking for potential readers. I believe we all want to make a positive impact on this earth, especially with others. This was yet another way to potentially enhance my legacy, making a difference for others in the form of another book.

As each concept came to mind, using a lap desk, scrap paper, and a pen, I jotted down keywords to remember each of my thoughts while my eyes remained focused on the road. I was doing my best to write without looking down at the piece of paper. Many of my notes were legible, some not so much.

Each day, after my long drive, I documented each of my notes in a spreadsheet. In addition to focusing on the road and traffic, these thoughts kept my mind extremely active during much of my two-day, 12-hour drive to Arkansas and also on the return trip home as the ideas continued to pour from my mind onto small pieces of notepaper. I documented well over 150 concepts, ideas, or tips that have improved my life. Once documented in the spreadsheet, I was able to categorize each of the points and I began to group and organize them for the structure of a book. It was not an all-inclusive list of everything that has influenced me, but it contains so many of the thoughts that now direct my life and have for years. These concepts might not all work for each person, but they sure have for me.

Functional Life Focus

These concepts are "daily living tips" related, not theology-based. They come from a functional, operational, and practical perspective. This isn't a religious or spiritual-focused book. That is another important aspect of my life, and I address it in *Turning Gray*. In *Gems,* I include a few scriptures that are functional-based.

These are General Concepts

Each of these points is a general concept, not an absolute statement that will apply in every situation. There are one-off exceptions to most things and yet I've found these concepts to be consistently helpful.

Not all these entries will be embraced by everyone. Each of us thinks differently, and we each come from different perspectives. Each one of these has resonated so well within me, and they have each made a huge positive difference, so hopefully, many of them will for you as well.

With each entry, I share a key point that has been helpful to me. It might be quick and simple for you to comprehend by simply reading the short, bold font statement. I then provide a short commentary about how I relate to the point. I often provide the source of the quotes or points so you can dive deeper if needed or if you are interested in more. The original source will provide you with additional background and context.

They are Simple and Practical

It's amazing how so many of these concepts are simple and practical, and yet I wasn't aware of them earlier in life. They are all doable over time, and most importantly, they are fully within your control. They can each help you as you slowly and methodically learn and then apply them, leading to building a new and better future. Through my having shared these concepts, I hope to be a significant contributor to your better future. Please let me know if certain of these thoughts and concepts resonate well with you and how applying them has improved your life. I would love to celebrate with you.

Many Popular Quotes and Concepts are Not Included

I've heard many other quotes and concepts during my life, things like "Better safe than Sorry," which is often true, and "Better to ask forgiveness than permission," which I might agree with in limited situations, or "Better Late than Never," which I'm not sure I agree with. Examples like these haven't resonated strongly with me, so they've not been included in my list.

Some Have Experienced Negative Comments

Some people have grown up with horrible feedback and discouragement from family members and/or friends, living amidst a culture of criticism, frequently hearing comments like: "You idiot! You're stupid. Dumb kid. You jerk. You're a waste.", and many other derogatory comments. I'm so thankful I grew up in a positive and supportive environment. I didn't have to fight through the feelings of inferiority and depression that might come from living in those difficult situations.

What we say to those around us is so powerful and can totally change the direction of a person's life, for the good or the bad. It can be like planting a seed in dry sand versus in dark, rich soil. The opportunity for healthy growth in the two environments is dramatically different.

I Have Shared These with Many Others

Over the years, sitting at a cafe with a beverage, I've shared these concepts with many friends and family members one-on-one. In my early 50s, I also hosted a small, intimate book club that met each Saturday morning at a Panera to talk through many of these concepts and how they related to our lives. Those were such fun and powerful gatherings.

Through *Gems*, I get to share them with more people, including many I've never met. I hope these can be encouraging, challenging, and helpful to you and others.

It has been so helpful to me as I've written *Gems*, helping me remember so many great concepts I've learned over the years. Some I live by consistently, and with others, I need a continual reminder. When you have heard or learned something once, it doesn't guarantee that you are consistently living by it. I need repetition and reminders.

Many of My Perceptions and Beliefs Have Changed Over the Years

Some of my prior thoughts, beliefs, and assumptions I now see as wrong, off, or at least nowhere near as helpful. Some were even hindering or damaging. When I began to plant the seeds of each of these new thoughts and ideas in my mind, my mind became more deeply re-engaged, stimulated, reenergized, and more open to so many more possibilities.

Many of these concepts opened new perspectives and a new world for me. I saw my world much differently, from new angles, with new and helpful insights. They were enlightening as each of them was revealed. These are now my deep beliefs, my core, who I've become and now am. It was so fun to read my first full draft of *Gems*. It was like looking in a mirror that looked right through me, deep into my heart.

I feel great when I'm living each of these concepts in my daily practice, and in contrast, I feel down, depressed, or low when I don't live consistent with them. I feel off, compromised, weak, and like I'm living in a contradiction. Living each of these regularly is what truly gives me excitement and energy for my future. When I live by them, I'm confident I'm doing things to help improve my life here on earth and that of others as well.

The Sources

Some of these concepts have been shared with me personally and have been modeled through others, and others haven't. Some I've only learned through the writings of those who have experienced them, not from my own personal experience.

As I share my list of quotes, ideas, and concepts, I'm extremely thankful to many of those who have provided them to me throughout my life, including my parents and siblings, other family members, and friends. As an adult, I'm also thankful to my bosses, co-workers, direct reports, book authors, audio teachers, video lectures, seminars, and special training programs I've participated in, such as the John Maxwell Team, Toastmasters, and the International Coach Federation. Of all of these, books have been my greatest source of help; as you will read, they've provided so much "Bread for my head."

The Structure of Gems

I've subdivided my points into twelve major chapters with broad topics, like Big Picture, Spirituality, Feeling, Thinking, and nine others. Some of the topics take more pages to cover, these include Thinking, Doing, Relationships, and Money. There are multiple subtopics under each of these. I hope this structure is helpful, especially if you're looking for insights about a particular topic.

Why Read Gems and How These Ideas Can Help You

I hope by reading *Gems,* you see many ways to improve your life and your future. These are proven concepts that have worked well when I've lived by them. I have experienced so many benefits from thinking and living by these *Gems*.

Engaging your mind and thinking in new, wiser, and more creative ways can help move you forward in your life routines or maybe even with some of your possible ruts in life. It can open you to a whole new world, seeing some things very differently, like the changes I saw when I discovered that paying down debt was a tremendous positive action rather than a dreaded requirement of life.

Ways to Approach and Read Gems

You can read the whole book, line by line, or you can just focus on the areas that you feel could be most beneficial to you. Another option is to review the list of major categories (subdivided by chapter) and decide which ones could be most helpful. A fourth approach would be to read one entry a day, which would take more than six months if you would like to have one stimulating thought to meditate on each day. Take advantage of *Gems* in a way that is best for you.

Only a Couple at a Time

I encourage you to only try to apply a couple of the concepts at a time, don't overwhelm yourself trying to make too many changes at once. Trying to take on everything in the book at once would likely be overwhelming.

How You Relate to Each Point

Here are some simple questions to consider in helping you determine how you relate to each of these points. First, read the statement, and then ask yourself, "Do I understand it? Is it new to me?" If not, and you've already seen or heard it, "Do you believe it is true?" If so, "Could it help you? Do you already live by it? Has it been helpful in the past?" If so, be thankful? If not, "What has limited its potential benefit to you?"

These simple questions can be helpful as you look to understand and internalize each point.

The Value of These Gems

The Fertile Ground of the Mind

We all have thoughts that have stuck with us from our experiences at a young age. They may have come from our parents, grandparents, uncle or aunt, a friend, and some we have read. They are stuck, planted deeply in our minds, and they shape our lives. They color everything we see, hear, do, and perceive. They are the filters that all our thoughts must pass through. They define the way we see life and ourselves. Hopefully, many of you are strong and positive; for some people, they're not. Like with a garden, we need to pull the weeds that are hurting us and our ability to be productive and produce healthy fruit.

Our mind is like fertile soil, it produces a crop based on what is planted in it. If no seeds are planted, weeds will come up. Don't let your mind be uncultivated. Realize that everything we plant in it will grow, or you will just live with a mind full of fruitless weeds. Our actions stem directly from our thoughts. Everything we plant in our mind will produce a crop, good, bad, or neutral. Be intentional about what you plant.

Each of these entries in *Gems* is a healthy seed that you can plant in your mind that will grow and produce a beneficial crop if you care for, water, and fertilize it. With time, each will produce a great crop.

Each of these points has molded and shaped my thoughts, feelings, and actions, leading me to a different and much better life impacting me, my family, and my friends. They can do the same for you.

A Raw Rock

Life can be compared to a raw stone or rock, which, over time, is sculpted by our experiences and relationships. Each of them chisels away excess debris so that what remains is a well-sculpted statue, image, or human. In my case, a man. Each experience and person we interact with has helped to shape our lives. These changes take time. As a 67-year-old, mature, healthy, extremely blessed, and thankful man, I hope that by sharing these concepts, you will have a tremendous jump start in life. You will learn significantly from my successes and failures, my education, experiences, and relationships that have taught me so much. I hope these concepts can give you a tremendous advantage over those who try to learn everything on their own through their own personal life experience. The narrower a life is, the less sculpting it receives; it receives fewer experiences and has less exposure to others and environments. I hope you see *Gems* as a special advanced course in human life that can benefit you without having to pay the full life experience price.

Learn Them the Hard Way

You can learn many of these concepts the hard way, through your own personal experiences, some successes, and some failures. Or you can take advantage of others who have gone before you, those who have already paid the experience price. You can benefit from what I and others have learned, their "aha's" and light bulb moments, and you can apply them to your life for your benefit without having to pay the price of the experience. It's a jumpstart, like getting the answers before a test, which will usually result in a much better performance, in this case, the test of life. Take advantage of this benefit for your own good.

Learn These as Early as Possible

The earlier in life you learn something, the longer you benefit from it as you develop, build upon, and perfect it to bring maximum benefit to you and others.

I've come to believe that each of these concepts compounds over time, and the more time they compound, the better advantage to you.

A compounding example can be demonstrated through the process of learning to read. It is great to learn an individual letter or even the whole alphabet, but that is not as helpful as understanding how letters form together to create words. A word is powerful, but not as powerful as understanding a sentence that includes many words. A sentence isn't as powerful as a paragraph, which makes and supports a key point. When it comes to learning and gaining benefit from a concept or idea, a paragraph isn't as powerful as a chapter or a full book on a topic. To take this one step further, reading multiple books on the same topic brings a tremendous amount of additional value that can be far greater than reading just one book on a topic.

I wish that I had had the opportunity to hear and learn so many of these ideas earlier in my life. It would have made such a positive impact in ways that I can hardly imagine. I've received so many benefits from applying these thoughts when I learned them. If I had only learned them 10, 20, or 30 years earlier, I could have gained so much more personal value and could have provided more value to others. I'm thankful for the life I've had, and the blessings I've received, and yet they could have been so much more if I had access to these concepts earlier.

It's like a person who graduates from high school at 18 and then college by age 22, in contrast to a person who gains the same education in their 50s or 60s. The younger you are when you gain the insights, the greater benefit you can receive for the rest of your life.

Thoughts Conveyed Through Words

I believe in the power of words now more than ever. I believe that the late philosopher Jim Rohn sums up their power quite well, "Words do two major things: They provide food for the mind and create light for understanding and awareness." I hope the words in *Gems* provide that amazing benefit to you.

It's time to learn some wisdom and tips for living an even better life from the gems that I've learned throughout my first 67 years. Your life is about to get deeper, wider, and better.

Chapter 1: Big Picture

Health

If you don't have your health, you don't have anything.

To some degree, I've focused on health much of my life, being reasonably conscious of what I'm eating and staying physically active multiple times a week by playing a sport, walking outside or on a treadmill or elliptical, or by riding an exercise bike.

This point hit home in 2018, on the day that I had my concussion. I even made this exact statement to a friend that afternoon before my incident. In recent years, she had been battling cancer, and I knew from my prior colds and illnesses, like my mini-stroke, that everything comes to a halt when my health is down or gone. In those times, my entire being was 100% focused on healing, recovering, and restoring my body to health. It puts everything else in perspective. Things that seemed so important suddenly don't matter. Even my spiritual life seems to disappear during the hardest of these recovery times. We must focus on maintaining our health.

Some people will give up anything, including their health, to gain wealth, only to later in life be willing to give up everything to regain health.

This quote, which I read several years ago in a John Maxwell book, hammers away at the same point above. It's so easy for our health not to feel that important until it decides to take center stage in our lives, telling us it is the number one priority, above everything. It's disappointing when we want to get our health back at the flip of a switch, and it is not that easy. It usually takes a lot of time and effort if we're able to get it back, and often, it never fully returns. We have paid the price for not paying attention to our health. Regardless of how we're feeling, motivated or not, to maintain our health, we must eat well, rest, and exercise. It is so easy to miss this point when we are young. We may feel invincible, but we are not, at least not in the long term. We must prioritize our health.

Time

His name is time, and he's coming to an end.

These are the words from a song called "*Time*" by Phil Keaggy. It sends a powerful message that time doesn't just keep going. It will come to an end for each of us. It reminds me to value each day and moment. I only get a limited number. Seeing my days as only a few helps me better value them. We all need to understand that our time is limited and that we need to be doing the things that we feel are most important for our time here and after we're gone.

I also love the instrumental portion of this song. He and his band go to town with their guitars, drums, and piano.

Patience

Patience is probably the hardest aspect of life, waiting, not knowing a result: tests, traffic, recovery time, and so many others.

This is a concept I've experienced repeatedly, just like you. Being content and patient is so powerful and is so hard to do. There is, and will continue to be, so much more "waiting" in our lives. If we learn now how to better be patient and how to wait, it will pay off for years to come.

When something is dependent on others, it is truly "out of our control." There is nothing we can do about it. It's best to focus on something else, something productive, while we wait and let time pass. If we don't, we are likely to create in our minds many negative stories and outcomes, and most of them won't come true. We worry for no reason. When we learn to master patience, we have developed a great character trait.

Our Nature

The scorpion and the frog. "It's my nature." Don't try to change or add to, draw out what is from within, that's enough.

I love this simple story that I read in *First, Break all the Rules* by Marcus Buckingham. I won't tell the whole story, but the point of the tale is that we don't change our core behaviors much. People who are introverts act like introverts; those who are aggressive continue to be aggressive, and so on.

In a manager role, this principle helped me to focus on learning about each of my direct reports to find places in our organization where they could thrive by being who they were, not by forcing them to make significant personality changes. Trying to change them for a role that was the opposite of who they were deep on the inside would be a waste of my and their time and talent. As a manager, this was tremendous insight and a major shift. When you find yourself in leadership roles, I encourage you to look at situations like this in the same way. And apply this concept to yourself. Try to find roles that allow you to be who you are at your core, not roles that require you to radically change.

Alignment

You can't fit a square peg into a round hole.

I've heard this throughout my life. Some things and people just don't fit with a particular situation. Just like with a kid's toy, a square peg will not fit into the same size round hole; no one fits well into every role that exists within a project or in a job. When that's the case, the best plan is to quickly determine if they're a fit. If they are not, then evaluate if they need better training and whether they can develop the skill or attitude that is needed. You can also see if there are tools that can be helpful to them, allowing them to complete their assignments more successfully. If not, it's important to make a change, hopefully helping them get appropriate feedback that they are not the right fit and, if possible, helping them find a role that is much better for them.

This applies to us as well. None of us are a great fit for every role. If we can tell that we are not able to or don't want to develop a skill or attitude needed for a role we're playing, we need to do ourselves and the people we're working with a favor and find something else. If we don't, the situation will likely become miserable for everyone, with less than optimum results. We need to be bold and make a change.

Looking back at the end of my career, I should have made a change much earlier. My heart wasn't in my role, and my manager could tell. I could have done the job well, but my heart wasn't in it, I only provided the minimal results. I even had a few cases where the results were below the minimum standard. I didn't care enough. I needed to move on, both for me and my boss. I hung on too long before I stepped away from that situation. I'm sorry to say it cost all of us. Don't let that happen to you or to a friend. If there is a square peg trying to fit into a round hole, help them make the change and find a square hole where they fit well. We can all provide value, just not value in every role.

Hope

Man can live about forty days without food, about three days without water, about eight minutes without air, but only a few seconds without hope.

I read this quote in a book quite a long time ago and it resonated. People need hope. I need hope. You need hope. When we don't have it, we don't have the desire to do anything or maybe even to live. Finding something to look forward to in the future is so critical for making it through the day, a better situation, enjoyable experiences, or something else. I keep a list of things I'm looking forward to on a planning document that I frequently see. I always want to have hope for a better future. And I want to be known for providing encouragement and hope to as many others as possible, including you. We must find ways to always have hope for our future.

Chapter 2:

Spirituality

Few of us are authorities on the truth. About the closest that any of us can get is what we hope is the truth or what we think is the truth. That's why the best approach to truth is probably to say, "It seems to me…"

This is a powerful statement from Jim Rohn. Again, it resonates strongly with my heart. It's easy for us to be fully convinced of something, and then we urgently want to share it with others as being the truth. The more I live life and see and hear the perspective of others and why they believe what they believe, the more convinced I am that none of us is the authority of the whole truth. I love his perspective, which encourages us to share our thoughts with others, but doing it in a non-authoritative way by first saying something like, "It seems to me…," or "In my perspective..." or "Based on what I've experienced or seen…" This orientation seems to be more accurate, and it sets the stage for an open conversation with another person. It reflects an openness as you speak. This simple twist is powerful, both internally and in interactions with others.

Hey, I'm getting dizzy now, falling to the ground in wonder. Hey, I'm getting teary-eyed, mouth is open wide in wonder.

These are lines from a song written and sung by Chris Rice called, *Wonder*. It's an amazing song that resonates to the depths of my soul and spirit. It reflects a true sense of a heart that is seeking God and all that he has created. It sums up how I feel. When I take the time to stop and observe our existence, our earth, and our view of the sky, I stand, sit, or even fall down on my knees or face in wonder. I encourage you to take some of this same observation time to help you put life in perspective. It has been powerful.

Love the Lord your God with all your heart, mind, soul, and strength. And love your neighbor as yourself.

This is a message from Jesus from the gospel of Luke, chapter 10, verse 27.

He answered, "'Love the Lord your God with all your heart and with all your soul and with all your strength and with all your mind'; and, 'Love your neighbor as yourself.'" (New International Version)

This has been a pillar in my life. The draw in my heart is to love God and man. It has been a strong foundation for how I've tried to live, and I believe it will benefit anyone who lives by it.

God has known every word that I will ever say before I was even born.

This comes from the Biblical passage in Psalm 139:3-4. Where it states, *"You discern my going out and my lying down; you're familiar with all my ways. Before a word is on my tongue, you, Lord, know it completely."*

This is an overwhelming concept. According to the psalmist, God knows and has known all about me before I say or do anything. He already knows it. This gives me comfort in that nothing is a surprise to him, and it also puts pressure on me to watch my words; he knows it all.

To obey is better than sacrifice. I don't need your money, I want your life.

These are words from a song by the late Christian musician Keith Green. It again is a challenge to give my full life to God, not just token elements like a weekly one-hour Sunday service or some money, but my whole life. It is a powerful and encouraging message that resonates with my heart. I encourage you to give your life fully to your loving Creator God.

If you can't come to me every day, then don't bother coming at all.

This is also from a line in a Keith Green song, *Asleep in the Light*. The message is, come to God with all of you; don't just give him a glance now and then, once or twice a week. Give him your whole being and heart. This, again, has resonated deeply with me. How well do you relate to this line?

Chapter 3:

Feelings

Feelings are neither good or bad, they just are.

It's okay to share your feelings or hear them from someone you love. Listen and take in what is being said. Don't judge them; just acknowledge that the feelings are there. This was a key message of a 1990s *Marriage Encounter* experience that Carolyn and I participated in. It was a powerful weekend for both of us. I learned I had many feelings that I wasn't sharing with her. It took quite a few teaching sessions and writing and sharing exercises to finally see my lack of focus on my feelings. I had felt like I couldn't share many of my feelings with anyone, including my wife, but after that experience, we both heard and believed in the concept that "feelings" just are, they're neither good nor bad, and we shouldn't be judged when we have them. We also learned how important it was to share them with each other. I opened up a lot that weekend.

Our last exercise during the weekend was to write about a specific question for 90 minutes and then share it with our spouse. I couldn't have dreamed of being able to write for 90 straight minutes on one simple but deep question, "Why do I want to go on living with you?" When it came time to think and write, I couldn't stop writing about my feelings. I went through page after page, writing about all my feelings on the topic. It was so powerful to release those feelings through writing about them. My writing time was cut short by the notification that it was time to stop and meet with Carolyn to review my writing and feelings. She was tasked with the same exercise. It was a tremendously powerful time for both of us.

That might have been when I first developed my love for writing about my thoughts and feelings. I loved that time and wanted more. Over that weekend, I discovered that learning about my feelings, acknowledging them, and revealing them was like peeling an onion. I had been living with very little awareness of my feelings. By thinking and writing, my feelings grew to be more and deeper, then deeper yet, and finally extremely deep and emotional. This concept was so powerful and has continued to enhance our marriage.

Feelings are neither good nor bad, they just are. I encourage you to realize and share your feelings with those closest to you.

Ask about a loved one's feelings, not just the facts about their lives. They go much deeper and are critically important.

It's so easy to live life together with someone and get into a groove of only being functional partners. You each know who is going to do what. You communicate about plans and activities and then execute them continuously and hopefully smoothly. But it's so easy to take the other person for granted. To assume you know how they're doing, how they're feeling on the inside, be it loved and cared for, or dismissed and unimportant. Through our *Marriage Encounter* experience, I clearly saw how, in many ways, we had become "married singles." We worked well together, but we didn't share that much about our feelings about our days and lives. We assumed we knew how the other person was doing. Afterall, we had been married for many years, and we had worked out so many kinks that had surfaced in our relationship. However, we can still experience a shallow relationship.

As I write this, I wonder how well I'm being sensitive to Carolyn's feelings today and how well I'm truly sharing my feelings with her. I need to rekindle that commitment to her, to again increase the fire of more and deeper feelings to a greater extent. It's so easy to fall into the logistics trap of getting through life. We all need to work hard to guard against that. It can remove so much emotion, joy, and feeling from life. It can make life dry.

If you only live by what feels natural to you, you would still be pooping in your pants if you were even wearing any.

I don't remember where I heard this, but boy, did it click. It reminds me that I must put effort into a number of things that I don't want to do or I don't naturally enjoy doing. It takes work to establish a new habit, otherwise life will become quite messy.

It's good to take advantage of many of our natural tendencies, but if we're going to show love to others, often it's going to require doing something that we don't naturally want to do. As teacher Gary Chapman explains, "I vacuum to show love to my wife, pure 100% love, because she knows I hate vacuuming. I only do it to convey love to my wife. And because she knows I hate it, I get extra credit each time I do it."

There are a variety of ways in which we need to move away from our natural tendencies, especially when it comes to displaying love and respect for others and ourselves. Don't go pooping in your pants in areas of your life that are important. Display some self-discipline and fight your natural tendencies.

Chapter 4:

Thinking

Perspective

"I've lived through some terrible things in my life, some of which actually happened."

This is a powerful message from Mark Twain. We seem to live out what we see in our mind: the stress of an awkward meeting, a fall, or shame from messing up a performance. When I create negative stories about how something is going to play out, I can emotionally experience all the stress, disappointment, and frustration even before taking action. It's crazy how this works.

Our challenge is to cut those stories off before they ever develop. We can do this by focusing on and acknowledging the facts about a situation and then by intentionally creating multiple positive scenarios in our heads, allowing us to feel those good emotions. Be careful about what you let your mind imagine; whatever it is, you will likely emotionally experience those feelings, and maybe even multiple times before the event ever happens, if it ever does. Don't create negative stories. It will cost you.

Especially with humans, life isn't very black and white, there are a lot of grays. The exception is natural laws.

This has been a recent insight since my concussion in 2018. Today, I see the world as nearly everything, as gray or multi-colored, nowhere near as simple, black, and white, or as one-sided. I am no longer fully confident in what is truth. I now appreciate so many additional things, people, perspectives, and actions because I see nearly everything as being a lot more complex. There are many more factors in practically everything. It has also made me a better listener and person. I hope I now see life from a broader perspective. It's easy to make things simple, cut and dry, black and white, just moving on in a rigid and routine way, but life is significantly more complicated than that. Unless we see and acknowledge that, we're going to have a harder time enjoying this life and the multifaceted people all around us. Life has a lot of grays. Be open to other factors that you might not currently know.

I read it on the internet.

I've heard people say this when they share something they've heard. The internet isn't the ultimate source of truth or knowledge. It can be helpful, but I don't rely on it to be the one source of truth to depend on. And I try not to share things that I've read from just one source on the internet, especially if it sounds unbelievable, surprising, and maybe even outlandish. If something is important, check additional sources and the original source. Don't believe everything you hear or see on the internet.

If someone is going down the wrong road, he doesn't need motivation to speed him up. What he needs is education to turn him around.

This comes from Jim Rohn. When things are piling up and overwhelming us, a natural tendency can be to try harder, stay with it, and go faster. Maybe, just maybe, that's not the right strategy. Maybe it's better to stop, look around, observe what is happening, and potentially change direction. Going more or faster in the wrong direction might only make the problem worse. Take the time to learn and educate yourself during challenges. That will benefit you more than continuing to do what you've been doing. You might need to stop, slow down, modify, or start something different. You might be missing the best solution. Speed is irrelevant if you're going in the wrong direction.

Some people will come and go no matter where they went.

I heard this in a cabin at a church elder's retreat. The discussion was about a family who had come to the church and had recently left. One of the elders said, "Some people will come and go no matter where they went." I thought it was a fun way of saying that in some situations, you don't have to try to fix it or improve something for someone else. Sometimes, it's more about who they are than what you are doing. You should just let them or it go. It's not so much about you or what you have done. There are many situations where other's actions or statements are more about them than about me or what I've done. In these cases, I just let it go and move on. It's not worth spending any more time on it or them.

We all live in our own little and very different world.

This is true for our relationships, experiences, and inputs. Therefore, our recommended solutions for others seldom work well for them because they live in their own different world with many different beliefs, experiences, and assumptions.

This insight comes from coaching. I'm fully convinced that we all live in a different world in our minds. We make different assumptions about nearly everything, and they stem from different experiences and memories we have, which are vastly different. This is why a reputable coach doesn't make recommendations to a client but rather draws out solutions from within the client that are consistent with the client's worldviews and beliefs, as well as their experiences and relationships. When a client comes up with solutions that are consistent with their life experiences, those solutions work much better for them. The client designed it specifically for themselves, with all of their personal factors being considered.

Based on this belief, I work hard not to provide solutions to them unless they ask for my perspective or unless I ask in advance for their permission to share my idea or recommendation. On occasion, I slip, but I work hard to help them process their own solutions and try not to fit my solution into their lives and worlds.

I encourage you to respect the life and experience of others in the same way. I believe it results in better relationships and often better solutions to their challenges.

Much of who we are is due to the actions of others, both prior to us and those around us today, in person, remotely, in government, through video, audio, and written communication.

This is a personal realization. I've made a lot of choices that have significantly shaped me, and…I've been tremendously impacted by those who have come before me and those who surround me today. They have all rubbed off in a significant way. How my great grandparents, my grandparents, and my parents have lived has shaped who I am today. The people I surround myself with and the things I see, read, watch, and listen to have a tremendous influence on me. I can't control my past, but I can appreciate it and recognize it for what it is, the good and the bad. And I can work hard to control who and what I'm surrounded by today, knowing that it is shaping me and impacting who I am becoming. We are not by ourselves on an island. Others have tremendously impacted who we are today and who we will be in the future.

What lies behind us and what lies before us are tiny matters compared to what lies within us.

I don't remember where I first read this, but the point hit home. It isn't the outside factors that are most important, but rather my internal perceptions and beliefs. How I respond is most important. And how I react is fully within my control. I work hard to keep this top of mind as I walk through the good days and hours, and the hard times. I must focus on what I control and first on my attitude and thoughts about a situation I'm facing. Am I thinking of dread, fear, injury, harm, damage, extra work, redundancy, and impossibility? Or am I thinking optimistically, with a can-do attitude, and about the opportunities to learn and expand my capabilities, capacities, and relationships? That choice is up to me, no one else.

I hope you're focused on what you control as you move through life.

Our Thinking

Think about these things.

This phrase is from the Bible and is also the name of a John Maxwell book. The charge is to think about things that are beneficial, positive, optimistic, mind-stretching, and healthy. It goes back to being intentional and controlling your mind. Not letting it go to waste. In Philippians 4:8, we're encouraged in the following way:

Finally, brothers and sisters, whatever is true, whatever is noble, whatever is right, whatever is pure, whatever is lovely, whatever is admirable—if anything is excellent or praiseworthy—think about such things.

Invest your mind in thinking about healthy things. Don't pollute it with poor, weak, and wasteful thoughts.

Be transformed by the renewing of your mind.

This is also straight from the Bible, a verse that I've heard for years. It is from Romans 12:2.

Do not conform to the pattern of this world, but be transformed by the renewing of your mind. Then, you will be able to test and approve what God's will is— his good, pleasing, and perfect will.

This verse has taught me for over 50 years that we change by renewing our minds. I've seen it so many times. When I see success in my mind, I can often do it, such as the ability to complete a new ninja skill, to fix a problem, to speak for an hour to over 500 people, and so many others. Changing my mind transforms me into a different person, one who is more capable than I had previously been. It is one of the reasons I feel so strongly about the concept of reading books and listening to powerful, positive, encouraging, idea-based people. When I see and hear things from them, in person, through books, audio, and videos, my mind is often renewed, and I'm transformed.

We must protect and continually renew our minds with healthy, strong messages and content. I hope you're striving to do that today, and I encourage you to do it even more.

Live and be guided by core principles more than by rules or laws. Principles relate to everything and aren't to be broken, like some rules.

This came from *Principle-Centered Leadership*, a book by Stephen R. Covey. He urges us to establish and live by principles rather than the details of laws, rules, and norms that are around us. He shares examples of how this works in customer service, using the principle that "employees are to be respected." When a customer treats an employee inappropriately, He believes it is appropriate to fire that customer. Living by this principle, the profit of yet another sale isn't as important as living this principle. He also shares examples where the principle of "meeting the needs of the customer" overrides a specific sales rule that might be in place. There are cases, based on unique circumstances, where breaking a rule makes sense if it violates an established principle. This could include checking out a customer with

14 items in a "Ten items or less" lane when all the other checkout lanes are full and long, and no one is in the "Ten items or less" lane.

Establish and then live by important principles for your life.

The wealthiest person is not the one who has the most but the one who needs the least.

This is so powerful. And it contrasts with the way many of us have been taught and what has been modeled for us. Our goal shouldn't be to have the most, to get all we can, to have more than others, but rather to be content with what we already have. When we do this, we are truly rich people with little, if any, need. It is a powerful way to live and it's within our control and is achievable. It is a healthy and wealthy way to live. Give this a serious try and see the benefits it can provide.

The mind is everything. You become what you think.

I've already made this point many times, but this quote cuts directly to the heart of how important it is to protect and develop our minds. Don't take it for granted. Take it seriously. It determines our lives.

We judge others by their actions and ourselves by our motives, and it should be the other way around.

This was an interesting twist shared by Stephen M. Covey in his book *The Speed of Trust*. He believes that we often judge and criticize others by their actions and what they do or don't do. Examples include trying to enter near the end of a long line of cars, showing up late, or blowing up on us in a conflict.

In contrast, we often judge ourselves based on what our motive was and what we intended to do, not on what we did: show up late, forget to contact someone, accidentally ignore someone, and so on. For us, it is okay because we meant to show up on time, contact them, acknowledge them, or whatever; it just didn't work out because we forgot or something else came up. We tend to judge ourselves by our motives.

Stephen encourages us to flip the judging process and judge ourselves based on our actions and judge others based on their potential positive intentions or motives.

This is a radical shift for many of us and I believe it is a much healthier perspective to live by, giving ourselves less leeway and providing more grace to others.

Abundance vs. Scarcity

This is quite a contrast in mindset, and both can dramatically impact our lives. We are usually on one side of this perspective. I grew up a "penny pincher," true to the example of my parents. I watch each penny that comes my way. My practice and tendency for years, and potentially still now, is to think that there is only a limited amount, and I need to do what I can to get my fair share, and not squander any of it. This is a limiting perspective and closes the door to so much learning and experimentation. When I see the world as plentiful and abundant, I don't hold on as tightly to things; I'm willing to part with them more easily, and I'm willing to spend more time and money to learn many more new things.

Our orientation appears in our attitude and approach to life. This is one that I continue to battle. I want to live with an abundance mentality but often revert to being tight-fisted, limiting my ability to grow and make an impact on others.

I hope you continue to grow in this area and see life from an abundance perspective. There is plenty for everyone.

Keep the main thing the main thing.

I've heard this from multiple Christian pastors. They have used it in relation to understanding the Bible. I think it's a tremendous point and I believe it also applies to so many other aspects of life. It is so easy to get caught up in the details and miss the big picture. I can care so much about how somebody is doing something differently than me, wanting to correct them or change them to do something my way, that I disregard or devalue the relationship with them, which is the most important thing. Keep the main thing the main thing. Don't get distracted by the minutia.

Endurance vs. Deliverance

This was a contrast that came to my mind and heart over thirty years ago while I was spending quiet time with God. I felt like He impressed me with these two words, and for years, I wasn't sure what they were supposed to mean to me. Eventually, I learned the message was that we personally grow and develop much more and typically better when we endure a situation or experience rather than when we are delivered out of, or from, it. It's natural to just want to escape a situation, to be out of it, away from it, in the clear, and able to move on with my comfortable life. But this view is short-sighted. When I'm delivered from something, by someone, something, or by God, seldom do I personally change or improve in who I am and my character. This message now says to me when times are hard, hang in there, stay with it, endure through it, learn from it, grow, develop in character, and become a better person. It is a strong and not easy message that is powerful to live by. I hope you will do the same.

If you think you can or you can't, you're right.

This is a quote from Henry Ford. I've found it to be true, especially on the can't side. Anytime I'm convinced in my mind that I can't do something, be it mental or physical, I usually can't do it. It doesn't pan out. I almost always seem to fail. Sometimes, this is the reality of my abilities, and sometimes it's only fear-based. I do have the capacity to achieve it, mentally or physically. My takeaway is that when I'm going to attempt something, if it's a reasonable stretch, I need to envision myself doing it successfully, truly putting my all into achieving it. When I take this mental approach, I'm surprised at how often I can successfully achieve something. Often, it can be helpful to first take some baby steps in that direction.

Our mind is so powerful it truly directs our bodies in either moving forward confidently or into hesitancy and fear. Keep this quote in mind and let it transform you. Think "I can" in more situations and see what happens.

I want to buy the thinking.

This was an interesting statement made years ago by a coaching client. We talked about how poor his follow-through had been on his commitments. He told me he wanted to buy more coaching sessions because "He wanted to buy the thinking." He wasn't fully following through on his commitments yet, but he was slowly changing the way he had learned to think during his first 30 years of life. He wanted to gain more of this new coaching mindset, being more open-minded, possibility-focused, and deeper thinking.

Our thinking leads to our actions. Improving your thinking will make all the difference in your life.

As you already know, that's why I've written *Gems*, to help you become an even better thinker about life and how it works. It will make a tremendous difference for you, just like it has for me.

Man is forgetful and needs to be reminded.

I came across this concept in a *Great Courses* lecture about Confucius, Buddha, Jesus, and Muhammad. It comes from the teaching of Muhammad. It is one of the core teachings of Islam. I believe it to be true. As a race, we seem to forget a lot of what is important. We might know to love others, but we seem to forget. We might believe that there is a Creator God but often forget about Him. We know we should forgive others, but we don't always remember to do that. Many of our core beliefs aren't consistently followed and lived out because we get caught up in the moment, emotion, and minutia, and we forget. When this is the case, it makes sense to build routines to help us consistently remember or do important things.

For Muslims, this includes praying to God five times a day. They don't forget because it has become a daily routine. I do the same by putting reminders in my Google calendar and in my day paper files to help me remember the birthdays of loved ones, maintenance for our house and cars, and follow-up with loved ones who are going through hard times or have upcoming surgeries. Because I know I forget, I use reminder systems to help remind me of important things. I believe we're forgetful, and maybe even more so the older we get.

How do you ensure that you focus on the things that are most important to you?

The narrower your view, the narrower your view.

This is from my personal experience and observation. The less our exposure, experiences, perceptions, and context, the less we're able to incorporate and include these factors in our decision-making. Another way to say it is, "The less we see, the less we see." This statement encourages me to get out, be, and do as much as I can so I have a wider and deeper understanding of everything. The more I see and experience, the more I can factor in those elements when it comes to thinking about them, making decisions, and taking action. If I had never seen a bike, I wouldn't know what a bike could do. The same could be said of so many things, a cell phone, a dating app, a drone, and on and on.

This also relates to getting exposure to people with other views. If I don't spend time with and listen to them, I don't realize that many people think much differently. Having wider exposure and knowledge is helpful as I seek truth and the right things to do in life. It also helps me better relate and communicate with others when I better understand and acknowledge their perspectives. My goal is to expand my view from my safe and narrow perspective to become a better, broader, and more educated person.

Think in terms of "What if I did know how to do it, get through it, produce it?"

This is a powerful coaching question for clients. It can also be helpful to us. In many situations it is easy to feel like we just don't know how to do or can't do something. In coaching, I lead clients to new perspectives, new creative options, and solutions. It is interesting to see how creative clients become when I ask, "What if you did?". When we ask ourselves this question, it opens us up to a whole new level of thought.

"What if I did know?" can do the same. See what comes to you when you think in this way. I think you will be surprised.

Thinking is one of the hardest things there is to do, that's why so few do it.

This quote hit me strongly over thirty years ago. It is attributed to Albert Einstein. It prompted me to start taking dedicated time to just "think," starting with a blank piece of paper and thinking and writing whatever came to mind. I would select a topic or situation, any topic on my mind, and ask, "What is going on with it? How do I do it?" and "Why do I do it?" and eventually, "How effective is it?" Then I move to questions like, "Should I keep doing it or should I stop?" or "Should I do it more frequently." Ideas pour in when I prioritize a quiet time to stop and think.

I started doing this with work challenges. This eventually led me to begin taking personal retreat times away to think more deeply about my life, not just my job. Eventually, I transitioned to what I now call "Refocus times," which are focused retreats, away and alone, to think about my life.

To share the value of these concepts, I wrote a book, *How to Refocus Your Life*. If you've not taken the time to be away somewhere, alone, in the quiet, to think, give it a try. These times have been extremely helpful to me over the past thirty years.

When we're not thinking about some definite problem, we usually spend about 95% of our time thinking about ourselves.

This is from *How to Win Friends and Influence People* by Dale Carnegie. It is a tremendously insightful comment. When I look at myself and what goes on in my head, this statement is correct and enlightening. I've learned that it is a waste of my time to think about what others are thinking about me and about what I'm doing. They're not likely thinking about me at all. Most of the time, we think about ourselves. This insight can help us eliminate so much useless internal, critical self-talk about what others are thinking about us. They probably aren't thinking anything about me or only have a quick, fleeting thought before they jump back to thinking about themselves.

One of the key points in the book is that when we spend time with others, the best way to relate to them is to think and talk about them. That's how strong relationships and friendships are built. This is a concept that I believe few people even consider, and yet I find it to be so true. We primarily think about ourselves.

How does this insight relate to your thoughts and behaviors?

Self-talk, the statements we make to ourselves and the questions we ask ourselves, direct and define our lives.

"Why me? I can't! It never works! Nobody cares!" or "You got this! You're doing so well. Keep at it. This is going to be so powerful. I'm loved by so many people." These statements, to ourselves, away from anyone, only within our head, can sound like an enemy criticizing us or an encouraging best friend.

Our self-talk is the most frequent talk we hear. What does yours sound like? Who are you inviting and keeping in your head, the encouraging best friend or a villain, your enemy? Whichever one it is, they are making a major impact on your life, much stronger than the influence of other people. And they're within your control. Decide right now who you want talking to you and listen to the one that is truly helpful and encouraging to you.

I've found this concept to be so powerful that I've added a segment to my daily journaling. I ask myself, "What should I be saying to myself?" Even when I've had a hard, challenging day, with many negative experiences and thoughts, my goal is to think in terms of "What should I be saying to myself?" What would a loving, caring friend be telling me?" It is incredible how encouraging I can be to and for myself when I take the time to intentionally think in this way. I often find that I had a much better day than I thought simply by responding to this question in my daily journal. If you're interested in learning more about my daily journaling process, check out *How to Refocus Your Life*.

Get control of your self-talk. It is extremely powerful in your life. I found the following book to be very helpful, *What To Say When You Talk to Yourself* by Dr. Shad Helmstetter.

How You See Yourself

You will never achieve anything more than you see yourself being able to do.

Like the quote above, this is from the Maxwell Maltz book *Psycho-Cybernetics*. He states that you will never exceed what you see yourself being able to do. This might not be a natural law, but it seems close to being one. I've seen this in others and me. When we don't think we can do something, we don't seem to be able to do it.

His recommendation is for us to work at improving how we see ourselves in our minds. When we can see success clearly in our minds, we have a much better chance of bringing it to reality. I work to keep this concept at the top of my mind, visualizing success in my head before I attempt something, be it a ninja move, a speech, or anything new.

Give this a serious try. It works.

Focus On

Focus on adding value to others in all that you do.

This came from my experience with the John Maxwell Team (JMT). When I heard it and saw it demonstrated, it brought me a breath of fresh air, bringing a gigantic smile to my face and satisfaction to my heart. I'm convinced this is the way to live. It is beneficial for others and personally to us. When we approach life and our days in this way, it changes what we do and who we do it for. When we consistently live with this perspective, everyone wins.

Make your focus on adding value to others.

Focus more on managing your energy than on your time. Not all times are equal; some moments have a lot greater capacity.

This was an interesting insight. I had learned a lot about how to best manage my time, but somewhere, I came across the idea that not all time is equal, and boy, is that true. In some moments, I have energy, am focused, am in a flow, am creative, and am quite productive. And there are other times when I'm worn out, beat, depressed, unmotivated, and mentally all over the place, the opposite of focused. Seeing that not all time is equal, my focus has shifted to leveraging my high productive, motivated times, trying to create more of them, using them better when they surface, and riding them as long as possible.

I find that I am more productive and have high energy time when I sleep a minimum of eight hours a night, wake relatively early, have a day task list and plan, can work in a quiet, generally isolated location; am not distracted; clearly know why I'm doing what I'm doing, believe in the actions and the benefits that will come from it; am well fed with quality, healthy food; and have exercised regularly and recently. I work to create this environment for myself so that I can experience more high energy, focused, and productive times.

I've also found that I am more productive and creative when I work on important topics early in my day.

These are the ways I've attempted to focus more on managing my energy.

Focus on setting personal records.

It is easy to compare ourselves to others, often seeing them as better than us and sometimes worse at something. I find the comparison game to be depressing. I often feel short of what others can do. I find that when I take the time to think about it, I'm often comparing their strength to my weakness.

Pickleball is an example. It is easy to compare myself to others. Even though I know that paddle sports and quick hand-eye coordination have never been my strengths, I still play them. I enjoy the game, but I'm not great at it. I can get down on myself about my play in relation to others or even my partner. Another powerful fact is that I play significantly less often than many of the other players. I might play two to six games once a week or every couple of weeks. Many I play with have played tennis, racquetball, or table tennis for years, and they also play six to ten games, from four to 10 times a week, potentially 100 games a week. They get so much additional practice. They should play better.

A healthy focus is on setting my own Personal Records (PRs), focusing on how I'm doing, not on them. My focus needs to be on, "Am I getting better at keeping my eye on the ball, not my paddle, the net, or my opponent; am I consistently in a better position on the court; am I more aware and intentional about the angle of my paddle when I hit the ball; am I thinking ahead about the direction and placement of my shot; and am I holding my paddle in the best way while I'm waiting for a return shot?" These are all things I should focus on improving, trying to set new personal records with my performance. Then, I'm focused on things that are in my control. I don't control how well my partner or opponent plays.

This might even be better explained with ninja obstacles. If my personal record is moving up two rungs on a salmon ladder, my personal goal should be to get up three rungs, a tangible result that I can easily measure. I should be focused on getting up that third rung, not on moving up and down the five rungs like the next ninja. I should celebrate anytime I make progress beyond the two rungs, even if I just get one side of the bar on the third rung; that's progress, improving myself.

Whenever possible, we should be focused on setting our own PRs. This applies to physical actions and non-physical moves, like how many sales phone calls or visits we made within a day, how many ounces of water we consumed for the day, how many hours we went without cheating on our diet, you name it. They can all be powerful PRs. We should put our focus there.

Focus on planting seeds, not on the results which may or may not come.

I don't remember when I came across this concept, but it goes back to focusing on what we control and what we can do something about, not those things that are out of our control and require the aid of others or other things.

Seeds are a simple analogy. I can prepare soil, plant a seed, give it sun exposure, fertilize it, and water it, but whether it produces a healthy plant is out of my control. I need to be patient and wait and see what happens. The result isn't in my control, only the preparation and the care for it. That's where my effort needs to go. And not all seeds produce a crop, it might be a weak or unhealthy seed. I don't fully control the quality of the seed. When I stay focused on what I control, I know I've done my best. That provides me with satisfaction, and often, many of the seeds do produce a crop. And as Jim Rohn says, most seeds produce much more than just what you've planted. His example is that a simple seed of corn will produce a full stalk with multiple ears of corn, each of which contains many corn kernels. We reap much more than we sow.

Focus on what you control; the rest is of no real value.

Choices

Each of us has just 24 hours a day, from the President to our parents, to our bosses, to us.

It can be easy to feel like there isn't enough time in the day to do all we want or need to do. But it's the same for everyone. Both for those who are successful and those who continually run into hard times. We all have just 24 hours each day to allocate however we want; it can be sleeping it away, watching TV, drinking alcohol, or eating. Or it can be spent reading, planning, doing, interacting, traveling, and learning, or in my case, writing. We all find ways to spend it, or I like to use the word "invest" it. The question is how we invest our time. I can't increase my number of hours in a day, but there are ways to make them better: enjoyable, productive, and impactful.

I won't share details, but I will share some quick concepts of ways to better use our time. We can automate an action that we have to routinely do, purchase tools to make things easier, or learn a new skill or technique that's better or faster. We can simplify what we do, we can shorten some things, or even eliminate them. We can delegate some things, we can leverage technology which can aid in the execution of some tasks, and we can involve others to join us.

What have you done to maximize your 24 hours each day? What else could you do? Chris Rice states in a song, "Every day is a gift you've been given. Make the most of the time every minute you're a livin'." Make the most of each minute of your life.

Good, Fast, Cheap. Choose one.

I heard this at work. It was a catchy phrase and is usually true. Seldom can we have all three of these. Usually, It's one, and maybe two, but not three. When it comes to any service or product you're producing or purchasing, you must make a choice. If you think in terms of businesses, companies usually have selected a niche they want to provide to their customers. Some restaurants focus primarily on good, both the food and service and they often aren't fast and are more expensive. Other restaurants focus on fast, and their food isn't often as good, tasty, or healthy, and sometimes they're cheaper and sometimes not. Then some focus on cheap, the food is okay, maybe, and might or might not be fast.

In my view, depending on my situation, I select each of these at different times. When it comes to something I produce, I've elected to try and prioritize my effort in the order of the quote. First, I want it to be good; then, if possible, I try to produce it quickly, and then also for less money. Usually, the good results in a slower delivery, and it often costs more due to the time it takes to produce it.

This is a healthy assessment to make when you're purchasing or producing something. Make the choice that seems best for you. Be intentional.

More than 90 percent of our life actions are decided at a subconscious, habit level, they're not intentional or well thought out.

Several authors have stated this perspective, and it seems quite believable. We seem to "just do" a lot. Many things have become habits driven by our subconscious. Many of these are great, like brushing our teeth in the morning, taking some daily supplements and medications, and washing our hands after using the bathroom. We do each of these naturally without having to think about them. These are all great and have been stored in our subconscious. We can be thankful that we don't have to think or work at them.

Other habits are not beneficial and need to be preceded by more intentional thinking, potentially in a different direction or action. These can be having another bowl of ice cream, watching one additional TV show late at night, starting our day by addressing whatever is right in front of us, or just going from thing to thing that continues to be in front of us.

We are much better off when we are intentional in these areas, and I say no to a second bowl of ice cream, don't watch another TV show when we should be going to sleep, and when we should be planning our day based on our priorities, not just acting on whatever comes up directly in front of us.

We need to be aware of how we live. If we don't, we'll live accidentally and miss out on so much we could have had and done if we had lived intentionally. When we take the time to think about what we're doing, especially in areas that haven't been as healthy or productive for us, we are creating a better future for ourselves. We have the potential to live better, more fulfilling lives.

Ability and Confidence

When we don't believe in ourselves, many of us first need someone else to believe in us.

This is from coaching. We so often need others to believe in us, especially during times when we don't believe in ourselves, and I believe most of us have these times if not many of them.

When we see and share our belief in others, we're giving them new life, new hope, and confidence they need to borrow during their low times. We have the power to make a significant difference in the lives of others. See the good and potential in others and share it. You might just be the one who is helping them take their first step in life in a way that could change their life forever.

As I write this, I received a Messenger post and video from my daughter Michelle, revealing that our granddaughter, Grace, at nearly 17 months, just took her first multiple steps. In the background, I heard "Yay!" and celebration laughs. We can make a world of difference for others.

Chapter 5:

Adversity

Life's Not Fair.

This is from the book, *The Road Less Traveled*, by Scott Peck. It is a powerful, in-your-face, direct, true statement that's hard to face. We want things to always be fair, at least fair in our favor. Reality is, it's not, or often not. The most deserving person doesn't always get the prize. We don't always get to the cashier first as we wait patiently in our shorter line. We don't always get acknowledged for something we have done, and maybe someone who did less is recognized. When we face the fact that life is not fair, it makes much of life easier to face, we're no longer embattled in our minds that something is not fair, especially toward us.

This is a powerful message to keep at the forefront of our minds. It can help us be more content with the way life works. With this perspective, we can quickly move beyond frustration and not be as bogged down and angered.

Adversity introduces a man to himself.

I've read this several times and don't remember where I first heard it. When we face hard times, we see who we really are, deep down. I'm working to focus less on adversity and concentrate more on how I'm reacting to it. Through this, I'm learning more about who I am, and hopefully, I'm directing my responses and thoughts in better ways.

Life is filled with adversities. What are they revealing to you about who you are? Are you pleased with who you are today when you face adversity?

A problem well-defined is a problem half-solved. Clarity adds so much value.

As a project manager, I've found this to be true. When something goes wrong and we try to fix it, especially if we engage others to help us, there is tremendous value in stating and clarifying what is actually wrong, and then what we specifically want. Rather than thinking or saying, "My computer isn't working. I'm frustrated."

It is much better to get clear on the specific issue. A better example of defining the problem clearly would be: "I can't get the Excel scroll bar to show at the bottom of the page. I want it to appear there again like it used to be for me."

When I'm clear about the problem, I'm more focused on identifying a helpful solution, and others are better able to help me. I had this exact issue surface a couple of weeks ago. I clarified my problem and then I searched for it and watched a You Tube video on that specific topic. It provided me with the perfect solution. This is one example, but it can apply in so many situations.

When you face a problem or obstacle, stop, and take time to define specifically what it is that's not working and specifically what you want. This practice can be helpful in leading you to better and faster solutions.

Chapter 6:

Priorities

If everything is important, nothing is important. Set priorities and limit your focus.

This helps me place my focus on what is most important. I truly believe that those who act like everything is important hurt themselves and the others who are trying to support them.

Focus is so powerful in helping us get something done. When we isolate the few things that are most important from the many, we bring true focus and importance to those items. It's also less overwhelming than when we see everything as being important. In some ways, maybe everything is important, but in relation to each other, some things are still more important than others, due to their potential impact on you and others.

We don't need more hours in the day. If we had them, we'd still fill them up and remain overwhelmed with our to-do lists. We need to prioritize the things that are most important and do them.

In *The Tyranny of the Urgent*, author Charles Hummel uses Jesus to convey his view about time and priorities. He states that no matter how many hours we have in a day, we will still come up with more things to do than the time available. The issue isn't time, but how we prioritize what we'll do with the time we have. There are many ways to prioritize activities. It's important to prioritize our activities, ensuring we're using our time doing the most important ones.

One helpful prioritization process encourages us to group our activities into one of four boxes. The four boxes are, in priority order, Urgent and Important, Non-urgent and important, Urgent and Not Important, and finally, Not Important and Not Urgent. The key is to ensure you're spending the majority of your time doing the activities in the first two boxes, not the last two. Then the second step is to prioritize them within each box, ranking them one through ten. Then, the goal becomes working top-down from that most important box, the Urgent and Important box.

This process can bring tremendous focus to our activities.

Select the three most important things, and get all of them done, before working on anything else.

This is related to the point above. I learned this from a book about simplifying life. The goal here is to narrow your focus and get things done. This one had a couple of unique twists that I really liked. You select three items or activities to work on, and you put everything else aside, on a backlog list somewhere, hidden from your eyes and focus. Then you prioritize those top three and then you work only on item number one until you hit a roadblock that requires you to wait, things like time to let glue dry, waiting for feedback from someone else, waiting for something you ordered to arrive, or needing a break before continuing with your deep concentration on that topic. Only then do you move to act on item number two.

You do the same with item number two as you did with number one, and not take any action on item number three if you can still make more progress on item number two.

Anytime the ability to work on item number one resurfaces, you immediately drop what you were doing and go back to focusing 100% on item number one till it is done, or you face another roadblock or delay with it.

Once item number one is done, all your attention goes back to item number two, until It's either done, or you face another roadblock. You don't pull in any other items until these three are fully done. Only then do you pull in three additional projects to work on, and you go through the same process.

This process ensures you're always focused on the most important and beneficial activities. And you get them done, not just started, which can be a novelty.

Reduce your inventory. It drains your energy and requires more maintenance and storage.

Focus on what is most important. Get the rest out of your sight and mind. I've always been a list maker, so I don't lose track of the ideas or things that I want to do. There are benefits to this practice, and… it can become overwhelming. This concept encourages us to eliminate from our view all the lists and ideas, other than the top two or three that would be most beneficial to us right now. It is decluttering for our minds.

To do this, review your long list, or stack of notes, and prioritize what is most important. Pick two or three you can work on now, or soon, then file the rest away, not looking at them again until you've fully completed those you've selected to focus on.

A long list can be overwhelming, and draining, and if it includes physical items, or notes and drawings, they're items you must manage. How and where do you store them? This concept recommends that you get rid of them, or file them far away until you're truly ready to focus on them. Which often becomes never, which is fine, if you have truly selected the most important things to focus on. Once those few selected items are completed, you can return to the list and pick the next two or three to work on.

When new ideas or projects surface, I make a note and add it to my hidden inventory file. I want my mind to be clear and focused on what is most important and right in front of me. I find I'm more productive when I operate this way. I'm not perfect with this practice, but I do use it a lot. It truly helps me when I do.

Implement the most important smaller chunks, faster, and potentially with greater impact.

I learned this while working in a corporation and it made so much sense. In a nutshell, it's breaking down a large initiative, or project, into smaller chunks, or segments, and implementing just them, resulting in delivering the key results faster and earlier.

It's like someone wanting to remodel a full kitchen, which could take eight or more months to complete. Breaking it into chunks might look like this. You look at the elements of the kitchen remodel and decide which ones would provide the greatest benefit. Then you work to implement the first few elements, one at a time. It might be that the kitchen is dim, so first replacing the lighting might be most helpful.

Maybe you're able to complete this in three weeks, gaining the benefit more than seven months earlier.

Then maybe the sink and faucet aren't working well, so you replace and install them. Maybe this will take another one to two weeks. Again, you realize the benefits months earlier. Over time, if you still feel it's of value, maybe you replace the countertops or the stove. You break the elements into smaller pieces and realize the benefits much faster. Ideally, you would have a clear understanding of how all the pieces best fit together before you take the first action, but once you do, you might spend less money early on and reap the benefits much sooner.

This concept doesn't apply to every situation, but it is helpful in many.

Stop starting and start finishing. Get things done before starting additional things and creating more inventory to deal with and manage.

I loved this *Lean-Agile* concept that I learned back in my corporate project management years. I learned about it in relation to business, with software development, but I believe it can also apply to many other aspects of life. It is related to the point I made just above.

It seems that in both business and life, it's easy to see something new, a new idea, and then we want to see how we can try it right now. It seems much easier to keep starting new things and not finish many things that we have already started, therefore we don't get the benefit of those things. Sometimes we never get back to finishing those things. With this concept, you look at your inventory of activities and pick two or three that would be most helpful, and you stay focused on completing whatever they are until you complete them. Then, and only then, do you get to go back to your list of projects or plans and pick another one or two things to focus on. In this way, you complete something and get to truly feel the benefit of it. You do it without the distraction of other things.

When a new thing surfaces you just add it to your backlog list and then jump back to finishing the few things you've selected to focus on. It is a much different approach than so many of us routinely live by.

He who pursues two hares (rabbits) at once, does not catch one and lets the other go.

This one is also another reinforcement of the points above, but it has also been helpful to have stored in my mind. I've heard this quote, originally from Ben Franklin, shared regarding rabbits, eagles, and birds.

Anytime our attention is divided, we seem to get poorer results than we expected. We need to be single-focused to truly get our prize. When our attention is divided, we often have a compromised result. The point is, focus on what is most important when you take action. When you can help it, don't attempt to multi-task. Multi-tasking can get a lot of respect, but I believe solo, or single-tasking, provides so much more value.

Chapter 7:

Planning

The Boulders First.

This is from Stephen R. Covey. I've heard this in story form and through a demonstration video. They were both powerful. I won't share the full example, just the key points and message.

A professor comes to a class with a large clear container and pours into it a full bucket of boulders. He asked the class if the container was full? Most said, "Yes." He proceeded to pour another whole canister full of large gravel into the container, and it all fit in between the cracks, appearing to again fill the large container. He asks the same question, "Is it full?" Fewer students agreed it was. He continued to empty smaller containers into the clear large container, next with small gravel, then pebbles, then sand, and finally with a full container of water. All the students finally agreed the large clear container was now totally full. The professor then asked, "What was the point of the demonstration?" They said, "No matter how full your life is, you can always find ways to fill it with more." He paused, and then responded, "No." The point is that if you don't put the boulders in first, they won't fit. Isn't that true with life?

Decide what your boulders are and always make sure you put them in your life first. Boulders maybe your health, marriage, children, family, education, or relaxation and recovery times. If you don't prioritize them first, they will not often fit into your life. The details of life will crowd them out. What a tremendous analogy.

Identify and put your boulders into your life first.

Planning proactively almost always provides better results and with less stress.

Planning generates much better results in nearly all situations. By planning, I'm forced to think through my actions, I live them in my mind first, before I act. When I plan, it leads me to establish a goal, which leads me to break down my goal into smaller steps. That allows me to sequence my steps into a more practical execution order, which allows me to estimate completion times for each step. Completing each of these planning steps enables me to set more realistic expectations. Maybe I had planned too much for a given amount of time and breaking it down helped me to realize that. Or maybe I could complete some steps much quicker, and I will have time to accomplish additional things. By thinking through the steps, I can also often see obstacles or roadblocks that might come up. Taking the time to plan also helps me better address them, which can help me achieve my goal more efficiently, reducing surprises or challenges.

I almost always get better, more intentional results when I take the time to plan. I believe you will receive the same benefits.

Begin with the end in mind.

This concept made perfect sense as I listened to a Jim Rohn CD. Thinking through an action in advance, ideally seeing clearly what we want in the end, maybe even feeling the emotion of achieving it, nearly able to smell it, and taste it, instructs our daily planning and actions. When we start with the end in mind, we have clearer direction and actions we can take to move us closer to our desired reality. Without the end clearly defined and understood, we can be aimless, unintentional, moving in many directions, sometimes with conflicting actions taking place at the same time.

Our personal savings and investment plan, which we have lived by for many years, was based on seeing where we wanted to be financially at age 57. We wanted to be free and retired, able to do more of the things we enjoy doing, like more time playing, activities like ninja and pickleball; traveling more and longer; visiting more with our kids and grandkids; and enjoying more time to do the things that I love doing, like reading, writing books, and coaching people to a better life. With this vision and plan, we were able to make tough decisions on how to invest our money, and not spend it all, or even worse, get into debt, trying to obtain material things that we couldn't afford.

Beginning with the end in mind can change each action of our day and life. Be intentional. Begin with the end in mind.

Define what you want. Be clear about it.

Many, including me at times, don't know what we truly want. We just know that we want something different, better, or some change or variety. When we take the time to stop and think about what we actually want, and we clearly define it, clarity comes to all of our decisions and actions. Clarity is also helpful for others who might be helping us achieve our goals.

General goals or statements are much harder to plan for and achieve. Clarity also provides greater motivation because we can see in our minds exactly what we want. We can begin to enjoy, in advance, the emotion that will come with the achievement of our goal.

If you don't have a target, you've nothing to aim for. With no target you can do anything, it really doesn't matter.

Having a target, or goal, impacts everything. If you think in terms of archery, with no target, you can have the tools, a bow and arrow, but there is no use for them. You can face any direction, you can be sitting or standing, without a target, you have no direction or motivation for any particular move or action, you are just existing, being.

With a target, you are motivated, you have something to aim for, a direction to face, a stance to take, and skills to develop. Your mind is engaged, and you can practice and learn what it takes to hit that target, or at minimum move closer to hitting it. With a target, you have a purpose.

If you find yourself aimless and unmotivated, establish a goal, a target to go after. It can be extremely helpful in leading you to live more intentionally.

We are goal-seeking beings.

In his book, *Psycho-Cybernetics*, Author Maxwell Maltz says we are goal-seeking beings. I've come to believe this is true for most people and situations. When we have goals, we live life and thrive and when we don't, we're stagnant and just existing.

Author Matthew Kelly reinforces this concept in his book, *The Dream Manager*, where he challenges us to write 100 dreams, or goals that we would like to achieve, and then he encourages us to share them with our family, friends, and co-workers.

Once a dream has been established, there is direction to life and often motivation, especially with dreams we would like to someday accomplish.

I believe we all need goals, something to look forward to, to strive toward. And I have found that establishing goals and striving for them is even more important than achieving them. It is the forward direction and progress that seems to provide life and encouragement to us.

Make sure you have established some goals for your day, week, months, and years ahead. They don't all have to be immediate, some of them can be long-term. It is beneficial to have both.

Mindstorming

This is a powerful concept and exercise. I was introduced to it by author and speaker Brian Tracy. I've used this process with coaching clients. It's like climbing a ladder; it helps you step up to a higher level of thinking.

You've probably heard of brainstorming, where a group generates a list of ideas and documents them on a chalk board (do they still exist?), flip chart, or an electronic device.

Mindstorming is basically brainstorming by yourself. You document every possible solution to a problem or all the ways you could accomplish a dream or goal. You continue this effort until you've identified at least 20 options. This can take time and effort, but it's quite rewarding. I've been able to successfully reach a minimum of 20 options each time I've used this technique.

I offered mindstorming to a client a few years ago and he said, "Yes, I want to try it." At our next session, he reported that he couldn't identify 20 options – in this case, the reasons why he was feeling much more energy since I had been coaching him. I was surprised, and disappointed until he shared, "I couldn't stop. I came up with thirty-three reasons!" This response brought a huge grin to both of us. He summed up his assessment: "To summarize these thirty-three reasons, I'm taking control of my life again and it feels so good."

As you face various obstacles, challenges, and problems, I encourage you to try mindstorming. To get to at least 20 options you'll likely have to raise your current level of thinking. Think outside your normal – outside the box. To get there you may need to include some crazy ideas that make no immediate sense to you. Just let it flow.

Mindstorming forces you to continually think at a new and creative level, crossing new thresholds in your mind. It feels great when you push through, and your mind is thinking at a higher level.

After listing a few options, you might think you've thought of everything possible and that there are no additional solutions; but I assure you, there are more. When you feel your creativity and flow are blocked, push through, and keep listing. This blocked feeling might happen again and again, maybe at solution number 13, and then again at 18. Keep going and feel your mind expand.

Once you have 20 or more options, you select one or two actions that you can tangibly take to move forward in addressing the problem or goal. Combining multiple options often creates a fantastic new solution. Perhaps combining options 2, 14, and 18 into one new idea will give you a creative new solution for moving forward.

Brian Tracy describes the concept in greater detail in some of his books, including, *No Excuses* and *Change Your Thinking, Change Your Life*. You can also google mindstorming.

Give it a try the next time you're stuck facing a problem or are trying to achieve a goal. This process can create stimulating new ideas that are lying dormant inside you.

Zero-Based thinking - What would you do now if you were starting for the first time?

Author Brian Tracy shares how making decisions using this concept can help get us out of a rut of doing the same thing, repeatedly. He asks, "What would you do, and not do, based on what you've learned and now know?"

Sometimes the answer is that you need to immediately stop doing the things you're doing, they may have run their course, but you've already given them enough time to see if they will work for you. It's time to stop those things.

This is a helpful, interesting, and freeing way to evaluate your activities. It's a way to face the facts about your current situation. Everything has its season. You can act at any time, but actions can be more productive when it's in the best season for a specific action.

Matthew Kelly made this point in *The Rhythm of Life*. He points out that a seed planted in the winter will not often provide much of a crop. That same seed, planted in the spring, could produce a tremendous harvest. Planting is productive, but doing it at the ideal time can provide much better results, be it establishing a new relationship, starting a garden, or taking on a project.

Try to find the best season for each of your efforts and be content with lesser results when you're planting out of season. That's the way things seem to work on this planet.

Never start before you're finished.

I learned this concept from a Jim Rohn CD called *The Weekend Seminar*. I love the way he explained it. The challenge is to see mentally, anything you're going to do before you start doing it. He gives the example of building a new house, assembling it mentally first, then on paper as blueprints, and eventually with physical materials. He believes it's foolish to start building before you've done all the mental prework, defining how you want the end product to look.

He also believed we should apply this concept to each day, never start it before you've finished it. Always start with a plan before you begin living each day. This makes so much sense and has benefited my life, helping me be more productive and efficient, feeling great about how I've invested my days.

Give this a serious try.

You cannot save time, you can only spend it differently.

I read this in a Brian Tracy book. We all have 24 hours a day to work with. We hear people use the phrase, "Saving time." You can't. Time marches on regardless. What we control is how we spend it, or as I like to say, "invest it." That's the difference maker. Focus on being intentional about how we invest each moment. Eventually, time will come to an end for each of us, a point in time that we don't know. We should ensure we invest our time wisely, generating the most peace, love, contribution, or whatever we feel is most important for our lives.

Break big things down into steps, and sequence them so as to not be so overwhelmed and to better help bring them to fruition.

This has been so helpful. I find it easy to be overwhelmed in so many situations. When I take the time to break down an effort into small pieces, and only focus on addressing one piece at a time, I'm able to make significant progress, and eventually complete a task that originally felt overwhelming. We can focus on and achieve small pieces.

The great news is that all big things are made up of many small pieces or actions. Focusing on the small steps, one at a time is the way to go.

Daily Match Your Volume to Your Capacity.

This is so powerful, and it's remarkable how well it works. I've often had a load of tasks for the day and felt overwhelmed by how many things need to get done. It's hard to be motivated to even begin to take on any of them. And I feel exhausted and depressed at the end of the day with how few of my mountain of tasks I was able to complete. Have you ever felt this way? I'm sure you have.

I learned how to match my volume to capacity from a factory production course I took many years ago.

The concept is simple. You define how much capacity you have for the day (hours you have available to do things) and then you fill your pipeline, or day plan with only enough things to ensure that you can get them all done. We only have a limited amount of capacity (time) each day to get things done during our 24 hours.

I have 24 hours each day, just like you. As an example, I plan to sleep for eight hours and eat meals for another two or so hours, I may already have two commitments, one with a friend and the other at the gym, which will take approximately four hours. I also need about two hours to complete a few chores and errands and I want to relax and spend time with my wife for at least two hours, so my best-case scenario, if nothing else important comes up, I have six hours of time to be productive completing tasks.

Often things will come up that will take even more time, so I build in a cushion of another two hours. That leaves me with four hours of potential productivity. I now know my true capacity for my day: four hours.

Rather than feeling depressed about the 30 hours of tasks on my list for the day, I review my list, identify the two or three most important things, and then estimate how long each of them will take. Then I only plan to complete the items that will fit within my four hours. For instance, if I listed four items, maybe number one will take 20 minutes, number two, two hours, and number three about one and a half hours. I now have my tasks for the day. I don't plan to complete item number four, I will not likely have the time to complete it that day.

When I plan this way, I don't feel the pressure to have to get task number four or any others done that day. I know at the beginning of the day that I don't have the time, or capacity to address it. Other items will have to wait for a future day.

By planning this way, I relieved tremendous pressure from my day. And, when I get to the end of the day, I feel great, I accomplished all I had the capacity to complete. This orientation provides me with a radically different feeling about my day.

Taking the time to assess and plan my day, "matching my volume to my capacity" always makes it a much better day. Give it a try. You will be amazed at how helpful it can be.

I provide more detail on this process in, *How to Refocus Your life*.

"Don't write it down, or it will happen! You didn't write that down did you?"

This is a fun line that my wife and I have said to each other, especially early on in our marriage. We learned the power of writing things down. When we talked about something, and idea, a purchase we wanted to make, a trip, or whatever, sometimes it would happen in the months ahead. Once the verbal or mental idea was written down on a piece of paper, it always seemed to happen.

I'm a list maker, and I love the feeling of crossing off tasks. It feels so satisfying deep inside.

If you don't want something to happen, don't write it down. And if you do want it to happen, take it out of just your head and put it on a list. You will have radically increased the chances of it getting completed.

What is your plan?

This is an awesome coaching question that I've used with many coaching clients, and I've also used it as an internal question for myself. It is so easy for many of us to have hopes, dreams, desires, and wishes, and yet not take the time to think through and develop a plan to achieve them. That takes work and intentionality, which is something that takes a lot of effort, that many will not take the time to do.

A plan doesn't always need to be detailed with 100 steps, but stopping long enough to break a hope, dream, or goal into three to five, maybe even 10 smaller steps, can be powerful and beneficial. It will usually move you forward toward your target.

Once you've broken something down into steps, it's easier to see obstacles that may need to be addressed, you get more realistic about your achievement timeline estimates, and you will often learn that the task is truly achievable, which can provide a surge of greater expectation and motivation to get started on the first action step. From there, often, it's like a snowball, gaining speed, momentum, mass, and power.

It is a great feeling to be moving forward and getting closer to a goal. Take the time to build a plan, it can be with a pen or pencil on paper, or on a computer, it doesn't matter. Just develop a plan, it will make a world of difference.

Schedule time on your calendar for things you want to make happen.

I've had many clients who have made great progress continually on their coaching session commitments. I've also had clients who have made a commitment, and then a couple of weeks later, when we met to get an update, I learned that they made limited or no progress. For those who haven't made much progress, I ask, "What was your plan?" And often, the response is, "I didn't have a plan." In essence, they just wanted to do something. So they made a commitment to do it. In contrast, people who consistently get things done usually plan and then schedule their action steps into their week. They block time on their calendar to complete those steps, like building a plan, buying materials, and assembling the materials. By planning the steps in smaller chunks and then scheduling them on their calendar, they protect that time for those specific activities, and they get things done. And when something comes up that supersedes their planned activity, they simply move the scheduled time on their calendar to the next open slot in the week, to ensure they still get it done.

When I take things out of my head and write them down they happen a lot more frequently than when I don't. Adding actions to your calendar can make a big difference in getting intended things done.

When will you do it?

This is another coaching question. It also is a light bulb question for many clients. It is often neglected. People talk about things that they want to do or hope to someday do, or even plan to do, but they leave out the "when." When takes an idea from concept to reality, to some degree a commitment. When our answer to the "when" question is next Wednesday, or June 29th, or at 2:00 p.m., we immediately start the wheels turning in our mind, now, for the first time, the clock is ticking, and we feel a surge of urgency. Now we can't just let sometime, someday, or whenever take over, we have made a commitment and we feel the need to get going with the first steps. Often, once the "when" is defined, a client will easily beat their original target date. Which is a fun, celebratory, and motivational feeling.

Define your when. Don't live in the vague, sometimes, or someday mindset.

Over-prepare and then go with the flow.

John Maxwell shared this several times during John Maxwell Team mentorship meetings. He was talking about giving speeches, but it applies to so many other situations. The key message was, to do all you can to prepare for whatever it is you have coming up, a performance, a speech, a test, and then go with the flow. Be in the moment and be you in that situation with the people who are there. Let the natural flow of your preparation flow. Be confident, and not nervous about the situation.

You will have better results when you over-prepare and go with the flow. I love it, and it has helped me in so many situations, especially in public, when I have the tendency to feel judged by others.

Chapter 8:

Doing

Act Now

The best time to plant a tree was 20 years ago. The second best time is now.

This proverb is an encouragement to act now, not spend time regretting that it would have been much better to have started or completed something earlier in life. Many of the quotes and concepts I've learned and am sharing could have been more beneficial to me had I learned them 10, 20, 30, and even up to 50 years earlier. But I didn't. I worked to apply them when I learned them, which was my only option. And I'm so glad I applied them when I did. I've still received so much benefit from them, even with my delay in learning them. Do now the things you know you should do. Let the past go. Benefit from them from here on out.

Jump and build your wings on the way down, but not if you're still an egg.

I learned this concept from Paul Martinelli, a former mentor and leader of the John Maxwell Team. This simple message relates to the point above. Don't wait too long to start or get going. It is better to get going on something and learn during the process, as you develop your skills.

This example is for the true entrepreneurs at heart. Commit to putting on a seminar, market it to the public, sell tickets, and parallel to this activity, learn the topic, and develop and practice your speech for your presentation. In this way, you're living by faith, selling something before it exists.

You might not want to go quite this far, but the general concept and encouragement is to act, which is of great value. Don't hesitate on the things you want to do. Jump, and build your wings on the way down.

Another former John Maxwell Team leader, Scott Fay, also helped put this concept into perspective when he shared, "Don't jump if you're still an egg or you will go splat. You need to have hatched and to have started to develop your wings to some degree." Just don't wait too long to test those developing wings.

Always start before you're ready, you will never be fully ready.

I read this in a *Success Magazine*, and it was shared by entrepreneur, Marie Forleo. Her point was that many people never start because they never feel they are ready, so they never start. The person who starts is always ahead of those who never do. By starting, you start the learning process. It is the learning process that's so powerful.

When you don't feel like you're ready, it takes guts to break through that fear barrier, but often it's the right thing to do.

Life is like riding a bicycle. To keep your balance, you must keep moving.

This comes from *Psycho-Cybernetics*, by Maxwell Maltz. It encourages us to always try to move forward, in some way, no matter how slow or how little.

We must do something to move ourselves. Sometimes my motivation and momentum seem to be non-existent. This concept has helped me find something that will push me slightly forward during those times. It could be, reading something new, contacting someone to demonstrate care, thinking through a topic that's on my mind, writing about something I've been thinking about, or completing a chore or small project on my task list. My goal is to get something started, that will move one small part of my life forward.

I hope this picture bicycle analogy is helpful, helping you to stay up and in balance with life.

You must go through one door before you can see other doors of opportunity.

I read about this analogy in Jerry Sittser's book, *Discovering God's Will*. He talked about people trying to find God's will and their desire to see a wide-open door, or opportunity, directly in front of them, among the many other doors around them. They want to look through that first open door and clearly see many additional wide-open doors directly beyond that first door. That's how simple they want life to be. At times, we, or I, can have that same desire.

He suggests that we're all in round rooms, with many doors around us, but often they are all closed. None of them have been opened, yet. And many of us just stand and stare at each of our many doors, overwhelmed, one by one, waiting for one to open, fearful that we'll choose, open, and go through the wrong door. In his analogy, when a door isn't wide open for us, we tend to just stand there, waiting, turning, and looking, sometimes forever, waiting for a door to open for us on its own.

He encourages us to first look for an open door, and then if we find that there isn't one, based on the best of our knowledge, pick a door, open it, and go through it. Once we do, we'll discover that… there is another round room full of additional doors of opportunity, doors we couldn't see from the first room.

In his view, we should keep opening doors, discovering many additional new doors that can be available to us, doors we won't see if we remain in the center of that first room. He believes God will direct us to his plan in the long-term when we move forward from room to room. Some rooms will include a door that's already open, and many may contain rooms with only closed doors, so again we'll have to choose and open a door ourselves and walk through it into yet another room of opportunity.

I haven't found many rooms with wide open doors, so I don't stand and wait for long, I choose and then open a door. It seems that when I do, I see additional doors of opportunity that I couldn't previously see.

This analogy has encouraged me to go through many doors earlier than I have in the past, and as a result, I have seen and had so many additional opportunities. I encourage you to do the same.

Actions

You're never any good the first time.

This is from John Maxwell at a John Maxwell Team live event. A member was asking what it took to fill a room when you speak to a group. John asked her how many times she had spoken in public. She said this would be her first time. He replied, "Don't worry about filling the room. You're never any good the first time. Just do it. Get started." His encouragement was to just start the process by trying to speak, so you can learn. His statement eliminated the pressure of being good. The message was to start, that's where the "getting good" begins. After you are good at something, then you can fill a room.

This has been an encouragement on many occasions. I just need to start. I needed to put in my best effort and learn from what happened. I didn't need to worry about being good yet, I just needed to be on the learning path to get better.

How can this quote help you?

People will always remember how good something was, not how fast you delivered it.

I learned this in my corporate job. There was always pressure to get things done, and now. Or even earlier. Do. Do. Do. I don't remember the source, but I came across this concept and it made so much sense. When I look down the road, a year, two, or more when others remember and think about whatever it was I was involved in, they won't remember if it came out at a particular time, on time, early, or even late. They will remember if it was good. My goal is to focus on the quality of what I'm producing, or providing, rather than the speed at which it's produced. This is a powerful perspective.

An ounce of prevention is better than a pound of cure.

Musician Paul Clark shared this in a song on one of his early albums. It is a simple concept of preparing in advance to prevent undesirable results. This seems to be a natural result on many fronts, including with the food we eat, our cleanliness, and even the words we speak.

I try to work at prevention actions to avoid needing the pound of cure. Prevention can be getting good sleep, watching my words, wearing a coat, or planning ahead.

From a health perspective, a poor result that needs a cure can be dealing with a lingering cold, needing to take medication to resolve a prior poor choice or choices I made. It can be having to apologize to someone after I made an inappropriate comment at a sensitive time.

An ounce of prevention is much better than having to deal with a poor result requiring a pound of cure.

Compounding impacts most everything.

This is simple and yet easy to forget. Nearly everything builds on what we already have.

Financially, when you invest $10 in a company they will work with your money, and over time, your money will typically grow through either: them making interest payments to you, a percent of your investment that they pay you for using your money; through you receiving dividends, again, paying you for using your money, because they made money with your investment; or through the company value increasing. When more people want to be a part of a company that is doing well, they invest money in it, which increases the value of the company. It might even grow significantly.

When you invest in ways where your money has a chance for greater growth, there is usually additional risk and you might also lose some money, in the short or maybe even in the long-term. My experience has been that over time it will grow.

This guideline also seems to apply to so many other areas. The people you know are often the ones who introduce you to other people, who in turn can introduce you to others, and it keeps going. Your contacts have the potential to significantly grow when you meet new people.

When you come up with a new idea and try to apply it, you will usually come up with additional ideas, and they continue.

When you try something new, it gives you a new experience, a new or additional perspective, which can alter your assumptions about many things you've known from the past, which can lead you to additional and broader perspectives about life.

Keep investing your money, meeting new people, coming up with new ideas, and trying new things.

Do the right thing.

I have no idea where I heard this. It probably came from many sources, including my parents, and you've probably heard it many times as well. Just do the right thing. It seems that we usually know what the right thing is, our battle is with displaying the guts, facing the fear, and following-through on doing that right thing.

Sometimes there is no one right thing, but there are several things that might qualify as being right or being good for a situation. In these cases, our goal should be to select one of those right options, follow through, and do it, even when it's hard and there might be a risk.

This message has popped into my head many times over the past 60-plus years. I hope you often hear this same message.

Honoring God through a life of integrity means driving the speed limit, 55 in a 55 MPH zone.

I heard this back in college during a church sermon. The pastor was talking about honoring God and living a life of integrity. He made his point with an example that each adult in the congregation could easily relate to. He said, "Honoring God means going 55 when the speed limit sign says 55." This was around the time when there was a significant focus on getting drivers to drive 55 miles an hour. I remember seeing many road signs stating, "55 Saves Lives." I took this to heart then and have continued to try to live by it for the past 50 years. When the speed limit is 45, I drive 45; when it is 70, I drive 70; and when it is 75, I drive 75. Not knowing the accuracy of my car speedometer, sometimes, I've driven a mile over the speed limit, and many times a mile under it. I know this sets me apart from a lot of others, but I believe I'm attempting to honor God through my actions, and a side benefit is that I don't fear the presence of police cars, knowing I'm fully living within the law. This action demonstrates my heart and helps me to live in peace in all things, including with my driving.

I just want to see you smile.

I heard this lyric from a song by Chris Rice, named, *Smile*. For years, my focus has been on living a God-honoring life, where He can see me, my life, and my actions, and can say, "Yes, you're imperfect, but on the whole, you've worked hard to honor me in all you do." So, my belief is that with a smile on His face, he can be thinking and saying, "Well done, good and faithful servant." I've tried hard to consistently live for His smile, each day and moment of my life.

Well done, good and faithful servant, you have been faithful in little, so I will provide you with more.

This is from the Bible, a parable in Matthew 25:21, where Jesus says, "The master said, "Well done, my good and faithful servant. You have been faithful in handling this small amount, so now I will give you many more responsibilities. Let's celebrate together!" [New Living Translation]

This is my life Bible verse, encouraging me to please God, my Creator, with all I do in life. At the end of my life, I want him to say, "Well done". A few years ago it hit me that I want him to be able to say the same every day of my life, and also each hour, minute, and second. I even named my business, Well Done Life, LLC. I conduct my coaching, speaking, writing, and publishing under this banner.

Out of sight out of mind. If I don't see them, I'm much less likely to be tempted by them: food and possessions.

This is so true and powerful for my life. When something is in view, it draws my attention. If it's healthy, that's great, but if it's harmful in quantity, that is not good. I've developed a lot of discipline, but there are areas where I'm still weak, even though I've tried hard to control them.

This is especially evident with food, and sweets, at home. When there are cookies around; or Rice Crispy treats with mini-chocolate chips; many other forms of chocolate; or certain candy bars; I face much greater mental battles, as I try to stay away from them. Often, I give in, consuming them at an unhealthy, but enjoyable pace. When those items aren't in the house, I don't have the same issue.

The same is the case with possessions. If I limit my time in stores, I'm quite content with what I have. It is when I go into stores, search on amazon, or leaf through a product catalogue that I start to desire things and move toward more discontentment, leading sometimes to wasting money on frivolous things that are of no significant value. The money could have been used in much better ways.

This is a great life tool. If you battle with consuming certain things, be they food or other items, don't keep them around. This strategy has worked well, out of sight, out of mind.

Sleep is the number one competitive advantage.

This is from former Ohio State Football coach Jim Tressel, in his book, *The Winner's Manual*. He believes, as I do, that, when it comes to performance, sleep is the number one competitive advantage. Being rested, refreshed, and ready to think and perform well, clearly, and accurately, is such a powerful advantage over so many who don't come into activities, events, competitions, and work, with the ability to perform at their best. It can be that they're worn out, exhausted, beaten, or trashed from recent prior engagements, living with less-than-ideal sleep, eating unhealthy foods, or using alcohol or drugs.

This one is significantly in your control. You just must prioritize it. Take advantage of it and get ahead in all you do by getting eight hours of sleep at night. I do.

Strive for many failures which will ensure a lot of successes.

I don't remember the source, but a presenter on one of my CDs made a suggestion that we ensure that we are producing failures, enough attempts that we're sure to have some of them. In a way, he was encouraging us to drop the pressure of failure and just stay active and busy.

Some examples would be in sending resumes, selling a product, looking for a solution, or for a location for an event. Our goal could be to make sure we've made enough attempts to get ten to twenty rejections or declines, and in the natural course of things, it is likely we will also have generated some successes, maybe even several.

We shouldn't focus totally on just delivering successes, be they sales, or job offers. We know we will likely receive many rejections. We should embrace failures, taking credit for experiencing them. By doing this, we are creating more attempts, or "at bats", as they would say in baseball, resulting in more learning and skill development. This usually comes with some success along the way, and potentially with greater success due to the additional experience.

This is an interesting way to approach a routine or repetitive activity that can sometimes tend to be discouraging and disappointing. Give it a try, instead of going for three sales, set a goal of 20 non-sales or declines, and see what happens. Keep going and don't get discouraged. Stay with it and keep learning along the way.

The Pottery Assignment

I came across this analogy in a book by John Maxwell. It is about a college professor on the first day of a new semester. He divided the class into two groups and gave them different assignments. One side only had to produce one great pot for their semester grade. The other side was challenged to produce a quantity of pots and not focus so much on the quality of the pots. The more pots they produced, the better their grade.

At the end of the semester, which group produced the better pot? Think about it. It wasn't the group that produced one great pot, but the group who produced the quantity, pot after pot after pot, unknowingly learning how to make it better every time.

The message is that by producing quantity, learning happens, and results get better. My goal is to continually move ahead and repeatedly try new things, knowing I will learn from each attempt, success or failure.

I just applied this concept again by producing a Heart of a Ninja T-shirt to market the ninja traits defined in one of my books and of course the books themselves. I produced and paid for one shirt and then promptly made significant improvements and produced a much better second shirt.

It's well worth it to try and learn, realizing that you might feel like you have wasted your effort, products, or results. It's not a throw-away effort, it's a valuable learning experience for personal development and growth. It's like paying college tuition for the learning experience. The benefits can be tremendous.

There is a choice you have to make in everything you do, so keep in mind that in the end, the choice you make makes you.

This is my favorite poem, shared by the late basketball coach, John Wooden. It is beautiful, simple, and rhythmic, and it makes a strong point that our choices create our future and who we become. Our choices are so important. We must take them seriously; they have powerful ramifications.

Make wise, intentional choices and decisions.

Think in terms of "How can I?" versus "Poor me, I can't."

In his book, *Rich Dad, Poor Dad*, Robert Kiyosaki, talks about the contrast of how we can look at challenging situations. In situations that might seem difficult or impossible at first, He encourages us to empower ourselves, and take control of our lives with an "abundance" mentality, challenging us to ask ourselves, "How can I?". This question can change the entire tone and outlook of a situation. A new world opens with this approach. This is in sharp contrast to the perspective that says, "Oh no. Not again!" Or "Why me, again?" Or "I could never do that."

Empower yourself, make the intentional, powerful, positive choice to ask yourself, "How can I?" And see all you can overcome, that you never thought you could achieve.

Track anything you want to change or improve; it will reveal what is actually happening and motivate you to improve it.

Darren Hardy, in *The Compound Effect*, shares that when we track anything, even without a goal, our performance improves. Simply by tracking something, and documenting the details of each time we do it. We come face to face with the facts that we have often overlooked, or over or underestimated.

Our quick glance at our life habits seldom reflects accurate perceptions of our behaviors, frequency, and quantity. We both over and under assume things are happening, that aren't happening. Like, I think I only eat 10 chocolate chip morsels a day, until I track them and see I've been eating 18-20. I believe I only watch an hour of television a day until I track it and learn that I watch more than three hours. I assume I exercise an hour a day most days of the week until I track it and learn that I only exercise 40 minutes a day, and only three to four days a week.

When we make these realizations and discoveries, we are motivated to improve them, especially when they are going to be documented. I want better results; I want to move closer to what I thought I was doing all along.

This is a powerful practice. Give it a try with things that are important to you. You don't have to track an action for the rest of your life, but long enough to: see the real facts, get back on track, achieve a goal you set for yourself, or create a new habit.

Travel early and often, while you can. There will be a point at which you will have less ability and options.

When I evaluated the possibility of retirement, it hit me that not all my days, the days down the road, will I be as mobile as I am today. At 70, 75, or 80 I will likely ache more, be less flexible, maybe have less muscle, be more fragile, and heal more slowly. As I move slowly to these ages, if I'm still around, I will likely have less desire and capacity to truly: get around to go see things; hike as long, hard, and high; stand as long; and go as long without rest or water. I will likely have less ability and desire to push my limits. This is the way life progresses, our bodies over time will break down.

My goal is to move, play, and travel now, as much as I can, while it's possible. Those limitations will surely sneak up on me before I know it, and many of the things I thought I was still going to be able to do, simply won't be possible and maybe no longer even desirable. Maybe, this won't happen till I'm over 100, and that would be great, but that's not likely. I want to take advantage of my mobility years and I encourage you to do the same.

Consequences

You become like the five people you spend the most time with.

I learned this through Jim Rohn. This relates not only to the people we spend time with, but can include knowing others through videos, books, and other written materials.

I've seen this in my life. Over time, I tend to use the words others use, pick up their tone, watch the things they watch, read the things they read, listen to the things they listen to, and perform the way they perform. Over time, we will likely pick up and apply many of their tendencies. We must ensure we're spending our time with people and on things that are uplifting, positive, growth-minded, and optimistic. We'll become like them. If these are traits we desire, that's great. If it includes aspects we don't want, then we need to reevaluate these relationships.

Jim even went as far as to say that we will make approximately the same amount of money as they do. It's just like our parents told us when we were being raised,

"Choose your friends wisely." It's true. And remember, it's not just our friends, but also the materials and media we live with on a regular basis.

You will be the same in five years other than for the new people you meet and the new things you watch and read.

Again, from Jim Rohn, and like the point above, who we spend time with and what we watch and read will determine who we'll be in five years and beyond. We will be the same unless we get exposure to new people, things, and experiences. It's so powerful to expand our world.

You become what you eat, physically and mentally.

When I eat fat, I become fat, when I eat sweets, which turn into fat, I become fat. When I eat nutritious fruits, vegetables, and nuts I become healthy. I guess it doesn't work here. I don't become a nut or a vegetable.

This also applies to what we consume mentally. By reading thought-provoking, positive, and challenging material, we grow, and over time begin to apply those concepts as we absorb them and let them marinate deep within us.

This also applies to the negative side. When we read and watch displays of anger, sarcasm, criticism, a "can't do" attitude, and little or no hope, they shape how we view ourselves and the world around us. We will likely start to exhibit these same characteristics.

We must guard our bodies and minds, only letting in healthy content through our mouths, eyes, and ears. We live on what we consume and digest, it changes us.

You reap what you sow. If you plant corn, you will get corn, not strawberries.

This has come to me from many sources, but it especially hit home from the book, *As a Man Thinketh*, by James Allen. It has also been strongly reinforced by Jim Rohn.

It's simple. When we plant a seed of corn, we're going to get corn, not strawberries or tomatoes. When I plant a strawberry seed, I get strawberries, not broccoli. What we plant, in both our stomach and in our head, will produce the crop that the seed was designed to produce.

If we don't protect the soil of our minds, or if we don't intentionally plant anything, weeds will grow. We should try to intentionally eat healthy foods that are known to produce healthy bodies, and we should be watching, reading, and listening to material that will produce productive, healthy, growing, and successful life traits, not things that will: discourage, hurt, harm, or create fear or anger within us.

We reap what we sow. This is a universal law. Take it very seriously.

You often get the results that you incented.

This comes from, *The Greatest Management Principle in the World*, by Michael Leboeuf. When we see those we're leading, doing things we don't want them to do, he challenges us to look within. This is especially true when we're in a leadership or management position over others. I've learned that the behaviors I'm getting are often due to the things I've said, or the actions I've taken. When I take the time to stop and think about what I'm doing, or saying, I often find that others are only doing what I accidentally incented them to do, through my words, guidelines, rules, or examples. When I realize this and acknowledge it, I can make a change that can and often does redirect their behaviors.

Do the Little Things

Doing little things well continually makes big things happen.

Former UCLA basketball coach, John Wooden, shared this concept in several of his books. He strongly believed that we should focus on the small details of life. He believed that when we develop ourselves, consistently doing the important little things, they will create opportunities for big things to happen. He proved this general law by teaching basketball. He taught his players to focus on the little, yet important, details of basketball and life. Those little details led his teams to win many college basketball championships. He taught his team the proper way to put on their socks, and how to tie their shoes, how to stand, when to lean, where to be on the court, and so many other details. These details became players' habits, which led to tremendous basketball success. It worked, over and over.

It absolutely works in life relative to our small details, like, when we go to sleep, when we get up, what we read, what we think about, what we eat, how we drive, what we listen to, and so many more. Making these repeated daily wise choices creates many positive bigger opportunities for us in life. Disregarding them can lead to a more difficult and challenging life.

Focus on improving your little repeated actions, not on the results, which are out of your control, and often good things will happen.

This is also from John Wooden. His focus was on what he controlled, which was the little things. Not in his, or our, control is the outer world, the other team, the other coach, and many life situations. He, and we, can't control how things go on the outside. His team focused on controlling how well they passed to each other, how well their shoes stayed on, where each player was standing on the court at every point during a game, how hard they dove for a loose ball, how fast they ran, and many other details. By focusing on what he and his team controlled, many great things happened for his teams, for many years. This same guideline applies to us.

Celebrate Progress

Create and celebrate all forward baby step progress.

We stay with it and continue to try things when someone believes in us and celebrates us. We see this when a child learns to walk, "You can do it, Grace. Keep going. You got this. One more time."

Encourage others each time they make progress. We need encouragement, so celebrate each forward baby step, which usually leads to even greater future progress.

Reward any progress toward a desired result.

In the 1990s book, *Whale Done*, I learned that in training an amusement park whale, how important it can be to celebrate any success in the direction of a goal. I learned that whale training uses a special technique, and that same concept works with people.

In whale training, a reward is received by the whale whenever it crosses over a bar at the bottom of the pool. Then, the bar is slightly raised, and each time the whale crosses above it, it receives another reward, more fish to eat. After raising the bar multiple times, eventually, that bar is raised above the water and the whale leaps out of the water to cross over it, earning yet another reward. The whole process takes place over time with many little steps of progress, all being celebrated with the reward of additional fish. Celebrating small successes in the right direction incents further action in that same direction.

Each time a person moves closer to a goal we should celebrate them. Don't wait till the goal is achieved to celebrate them. Celebrate them early and often, when any movement is made in the right direction. We love to be encouraged and celebrated, even with our smaller successes.

Endurance

The power of the word "Yet."

This comes from my book, *The Heart of a Ninja*. Training as a ninja warrior, I've learned the tremendous power in thinking, and especially in verbalizing, the word, "yet", in reference to things we are not currently able to do. By saying this powerful word, we open a whole new world of possibility, that there is now a chance, the hope, that someday we might achieve our goal. This applies to all aspects of life.

When you're facing a challenge, I encourage you to modify your mental and verbal statements from "I can't" or "I will never be able to," by adding the powerful word, "Yet." and watch the new perspective and possibilities begin.

It isn't easy to make this transition, especially when it comes to speaking the words, but when we do, we have acknowledged a new level of possibility. Use the word "yet" often, especially with your greatest challenges.

Chapter 9:

Personal Growth

Development

If nothing changes, nothing changes.

This comes from a book by former NBA basketball player and coach, Avery Johnson. It is the simplest way to say what each of the next few quotes also convey. I like them all, but this one is more direct. He states, "If nothing changes, nothing changes." Simply, if you want a different result, you must change something you're doing. If you don't, you will get the same results you've been getting. It is so clear, sharp, and to the point. I love this one. It is worth chewing on for a while. It is so true.

The definition of insanity is doing the same thing and expecting a different result.

This description takes more words to convey the same point. Why do we want and hope for better results when we're not willing to change the things we do, and to some degree we all do it. If we want something to change we need to change something or things. Some of my friends, who know this concept have encouraged or challenged each other with the simple line, "You know the definition of insanity."

If the same man is bitten by the same dog the second time, it's time to shoot… the man.

I heard this a long time ago and for some reason, it has resonated strongly with me. The point is the same, but it directs us to look internally, and not blame outward situations or people. We need to learn from our experiences and make the appropriate changes, so we get better results going forward. It's up to us.

A lesson is repeated until it's learned.

When I have shared this with an audience in a speech, I say it slowly, with a smile, twice. It's so powerful. It takes time to truly absorb. The same things keep happening to us until we do something different to change them.

Sometimes, the issue is that we don't know that we need to change, or don't know what to change, and other times we know, but aren't willing to make that change. When we don't, we experience the same poor result. When we see a result that we don't like, and it happens repeatedly, this is a clear reminder to look internally and see what we are doing that is likely causing the undesirable situation. We haven't yet learned the lesson until we make the change.

Can you relate? I think you probably can.

If you find yourself in a hole, stop digging.

This is the final quote that relates to the same core message. As you can see, I need a lot of reminders and perspectives to help me consistently apply this general concept.

This one comes from Will Rogers. Many people can probably relate to this. No one wants to be stuck in a hole. When we don't stop to think about what is going on, and how we can improve a situation, many of us just keep our heads down and work even harder as we keep digging our hole even deeper. It doesn't seem to come naturally to stop and think. We just keep digging deeper and deeper into the hole, thinking we're doing all we can to resolve the problem. Usually, that's not the case. We need to stop, get a broader perspective, and do something differently to allow a change to begin to happen.

Invest in yourself, it's the greatest investment and it won't be impacted by inflation or taxes.

This is a great perspective. Spending time and money on myself, to grow me, to invest in me, is the greatest investment I can make. It will pay dividends for years, over and over.

When we learn something new, a new skill, it will not lose value due to inflation as prices increase. The pay for performing the skill will normally grow with inflation, and there is no tax on your skill. You get the full benefit of it.

To some degree, I've focused on developing my skills all my life, but I wish I had been even more intentional and invested even more in my development, especially since I graduated from college.

It is normal for many of us to complete high school or college, get our education, hopefully, learn a lot, and then feel like we have completed the primary learning phase of our lives. Now, I believe that our focus on learning should continue, all the way up to our death. Continual learning is beneficial for our brains and for the practical side of life.

Always keep investing in yourself.

Operate like a guided missile, moving forward, getting feedback, adjusting, and moving forward some more. Do this continually both for fixed and especially for moving targets or goals.

This is another analogy from, *Psycho-Cybernetics*, about how to live. I believe it's the best way to hit targets or goals in life. Operating like a guided missile is the best and easiest way to achieve goals. It has a set target, continually receives feedback, and then makes frequent minor adjustments toward that goal, a goal that might even be moving based on outside factors.

This contrasts with being rigid with our initial aim and missing a target by a wide margin, or by having to make major, often painful, shifts or changes along the way.

This analogy has helped me to be open to receiving feedback and making appropriate smaller changes along the way. It can do the same for you.

Sharpen the ax.

This is by author, Stephen R. Covey, from his book, *The 7 Habits of Highly Effective People*, which is a great read.

He shares a story of a person working hard to cut down trees in a forest, but his ax is dull, requiring many more swings, and additional effort to complete the job. By simply stopping, taking out a sharpening stone, and sharpening his ax. The individual loses time while sharpening the ax, but gains so much more progress as he returns to cutting down the trees, finding that they fall much faster with a sharp ax.

Make sure your ax is sharp. For you, being sharp might mean being rested, refreshed, being better educated about how to do something, or finding a better tool to support you. Taking the time to sharpen yourself can make your work and effort much more productive. Take excellent care of your ax, you.

Once you stop learning, you start dying.

This is by Albert Einstein. I've found it to be true, even at the smallest level. When I don't feel like I'm learning, I feel dead on the inside. I'm down, unmotivated, and sometimes even depressed. There is something about learning something new, something I didn't previously know, that miraculously sends a surge of energy through my being, increasing my hope for more possibilities and more learning. I gain a hunger for even more.

I personally need to be continually learning, and it sure helps to be learning something I'm interested in. How about you? Can you relate? What are you currently learning? Hopefully, you're learning some great new life concepts as you continue to read and consume *Gems*.

Work harder on yourself than you do on your job. Work hard on your job and you will make a good living. Work hard on yourself and you will make a fortune.

This is a Jim Rohn classic. Unfortunately, I didn't learn this concept until the last few years of my work career. I worked hard on my job, and only casually on myself, not all that intentionally.

I grew but in a slow and limited way. When I grew up, it was often due to external circumstances, changes required at work, programs that were being implemented, or courses that were required.

Ironically, in my first ten years of work, one of my responsibilities was management of the company's Personal Development materials library, where employees could check out materials on leadership, management, communication, project management, and many other topics. I didn't take advantage of these materials because I had not heard or understood this concept and perspective.

I did well and was quite blessed during my full-time working career, but I'm convinced I would have had even better results had I employed this view earlier in my 33-year corporate career.

We should work hard at our job, but we should work even harder on ourselves which can result in so many additional long-term skills that can, and will, pay off for years, regardless of the topic: communication, leadership, management, technology, processes, you name it. They can all significantly enhance our ability to perform, for ourselves and others.

The more value you bring to the marketplace, the more financial rewards you will receive.

If a man empties his purse into his head, no man can take it away from him. An investment in knowledge always pays the best interest.

This comes from Benjamin Franklin. He encouraged us to spend money on improving our thinking, knowledge, and wisdom. He believed it's the best way to use our money and that it pays the best interest. When you invest in yourself, grow, and develop yourself, no one can steal it or take it away.

When you learn how to type, you have developed a skill that's yours. When you learn how to invest money, you have the knowledge of how to invest for the rest of your life. When you learn how to plan your day to make it more productive, you can take advantage of that skill each day forward. When you learn how to better communicate it will impact all your interactions for the rest of your life.

Invest in you. No one can take those new skills away.

When you plant something, anything, the initial growth is down, developing the roots, and this is prior to any visible growth of a stem, leaves, and especially before any produce or fruit.

This helps me so much with being patient. I like things to happen quickly, no matter what it is. The analogy of a plant helps me understand and remember that everything is a process and that growth usually happens downward or inward before the upward and out, and when it produces a crop.

To learn to play the guitar, I couldn't just pick it up, spend ten minutes or ten hours practicing, and automatically be able to play to the delight of large crowds. First, the roots had to grow, I had to learn how to play individual notes and chords, I had to build up the toughness and calluses on my fingers, and I had to learn how to pick the strings and strum to the designated timing. And there were many other root development elements that had to be developed before I was able to play a song, poorly, and just for myself. With significant time and effort, over months and years, those strong roots could produce a pleasant sound, even for others.

This is the same with so many other situations, finding a job, making a sale, and learning any new skill. The work must be put in to develop a strong root system well before there is a crop.

Be patient with the growth process. It takes time and effort.

Not reading is like not having the ability to read.

This is from Jim Rohn. I wasn't much of a reader during my first 40 years of life. I missed out on so much learning, from both non-fiction and fiction books. I could have had exposure to so much more, beyond the walls of our house and my standard life routines. I could have learned much more, earlier in life.

Not reading is like not having the ability to read. Read as much and as often as you can. It will give you a tremendous advantage in life, especially over those who were like me, the non-readers.

The book you don't read won't help you.

This is another line from Jim Rohn. It is another way of saying the same thing. Take the time and prioritize reading, listening, and learning. It can't help you if you don't read it or hear it. Invest in your development.

We need bread for the head.

This is a fun catchy line from Jim Rohn, "Bread for the Head." He is referring to books and ideas being fed into our minds. He's convinced that we all need to feed our minds with healthy content, just like we need to eat healthy food for our bodies.

How well are you providing bread for your head? It needs nutrition too. Read powerful, mind-stretching books, like this one.

It isn't what the book costs; it's what it will cost if you don't read it.

I love this perspective, now that I love to read books and learn new concepts. Jim Rohn emphasizes the cost of not learning, from seminars, blogs, books, YouTube videos, webcasts, magazines, or whatever the source.

The biggest cost to us is not having a broader perspective on life and opportunities. It isn't the expense of the $15 or $25 book, or the $800 course. It's important to understand the cost of not learning how to be more and provide more value to our family, friends, customers, and bosses.

The more value we learn to provide to others, typically the better we are rewarded by our companies and customers. We are given the opportunities to play bigger and greater influential roles, which often come with greater pay and benefits.

Read, listen, and absorb all you can, about life and work, and about things you aren't already familiar with. Often the best ideas come from exposure to things we don't already know much about.

Give a man a fish and feed him for the day. Teach a man to fish and feed him for a lifetime.

This is by Stephen R. Covey. It immediately resonated in my mind and heart. It's much better to help someone learn something, and even better, to learn how to learn things, than to just provide them with something to meet an urgent or immediate need. It isn't that urgent needs are irrelevant. People need food, water, clothing, and protection, but in addition to these things, the best gift is to help them learn ways to prevent or limit difficult situations in the future.

As a coach, I love my add-on, which is to help them learn "how to learn themselves," which in my mind is the ultimate gift.

Skills

Learn to Speed Read

I learned to read in school, just like you. But I didn't like reading, I read because it was required.

When reading scripture with Carolyn, she wanted to turn the page while I was still reading at the bottom of the second column of text on the first page. This example taught me that she read a whole lot faster than me. I needed to learn to read faster. We called my paper mail stack, my "black hole." Things would go in that stack and never come out as I would fall even farther behind in reading.

In my early thirties, I purchased and took an audio cassette tape speed-reading course. From it, I learned that I read at about a third of Carolyn's speed and that she also retained the content much better. I didn't understand how that could be, and I wanted to develop that level of reading skill.

I won't teach you all the concepts, but by applying several of them, I was able to more than double my reading speed, which also improved my comprehension and retention. I went from reading 178 to closer to 250 words a minute. It hadn't matched Carolyn's 400+ words, but I was much, much faster than I had been. I loved it and was able to eliminate my black hole. This enhanced skill helped me in so many ways.

A few of the key concepts included: developing and controlling my eye movement, eliminating my subvocalization, letting my fingers direct my eyes, and practicing reading faster than I think I can comprehend. These all made a significant difference.

If you're a slower reader, try a speed-reading course. You might be amazed at the results. It could open a whole new world for you.

Chapter 10:

Relationships

Others

The deepest urge in human nature is the "desire to be important."

This comes from the Dale Carnegie book, *How to Win Friends and Influence People*. Relationships are so much better when we keep this in mind. Helping others feel important can and does change the dynamic of any relationship.

Apply this in all your relationships. It will change them, and you.

Do unto others as you would have them do unto you.

This is from the Bible. It is referred to as the "Golden Rule." It's Luke 6:31. It is stated by Jesus. It simply means, to treat others the way you would want to be treated. It is a common courtesy approach to life, and in my experience, it's an excellent practice for both the giver and the receiver. It is a win-win approach to life.

The Speed of Trust

This is the title of a book by Stephen M. Covey. When trust exists between people or groups of people, everything is easier, faster, and better.

He makes his point in many practical ways. One example is airline safety since 9/11. When our trust in air travel safety eroded, everything slowed down. New and extra safeguards and rules were implemented, the checking of luggage became more detailed and complex, and more ID was required. All due to the reduced trust level.

This is also the case with personal relationships. When you highly trust someone, everything feels easy, fast, and more enjoyable. When you're betrayed, or trust is lost, more caution kicks in, making everything harder, more challenging, more stressful, and slower.

My goal is to earn trust from others, and I also try to build relationships with people I can trust. Living without trust is a hard and ugly way to live.

Same Team!

This is a phrase I used with our family when the kids were growing up at home. The rest of our family seems to enjoy debate, or what I see as arguing, a lot more than I do. I often see arguments as divisive, family members being defensive with one another. I know every personality is different, but for who I am, at times I would chime in, "Same team!" I did this wanting to ensure that we were all striving for the same goal or result.

It is easy to get defensive about something we have said, we don't like to be wrong, but sometimes that perspective can lead us to attack another person's perspective or even them. At times, it is good to be reminded that in the end, we are on the same team. We shouldn't waste too much time arguing about things that don't matter, just because we want to be right.

Keep this concept in mind the next time you start to feel defensive about a statement someone said to you, especially when it is in regard to something you have said. Make sure your response doesn't compromise the fact that you are both on the same team, you really want what is best for both or all of you.

People almost always have a reason for doing what they do.

Even when we do things that are harmful to us or others, we seem to rationalize our actions, telling ourselves that the action is right, at least in the moment. If we weren't convinced of that, we probably wouldn't do it.

I might sneak a cookie since I really like the taste, and I believe it will be sweet on my tongue, even though it might be unhealthy. We seem to do a lot for what we believe to be "good reasons". Our good reasons just might not seem like a good reason to others, and they may not actually be good for us in the long term.

When we assume others have a good reason for their actions, it helps us to be more patient and forgiving, and it can lead us to try and understand why they thought an action would be good for them or someone they love. There is often a motive or assumption that I may not be aware of. This isn't to justify our or their actions, but this outlook can help us better understand ourselves and others, and potentially help us to better act and respond.

Try approaching both your actions, and looking at the actions of others, from this perspective.

People would much rather react to a draft, or proposal than be asked a general open-ended question.

Most people respond better to something when they have something to react to. Especially when it's in writing.

If I ask someone what they would like to do for the day, many will not be sure how to respond. However, if I offer a list of a few options and provide them with a proposed order and with some general timing, I find they can give me immediate helpful detailed feedback that will make for a much better plan. They might say, "I'd rather not do the second item at all, and can we do your fourth item first? I usually enjoy that earlier in the day." Input like this can make for a much more enjoyable day.

General, blanket, fully open-ended questions don't generally provide anywhere near as helpful information. Consider providing others with something to react to. It has paid off well and I believe it can do the same for you.

Communication - Listening

Assume innocence.

This came from a Bank One training program called, "Be the One". The challenge was for us to assume innocence with others and their actions, not start with the assumption of guilt on their part.

A simple example is the highway driver who cuts in front of us on a crowded exit. Many of us may assume that person is a real jerk, a person who's full of themselves, someone who thinks the rules of etiquette don't apply to them. Assuming innocence is saying to ourselves, "I don't know why they cut in front of me. Maybe they're unfamiliar with this highway and exit and just discovered they needed to get off. Maybe they're from out of town and are unfamiliar with these roads. Maybe they're facing an emergency and need some type of immediate attention. Or maybe they were distracted while driving and just about missed the exit, only realizing it at the end. Many of us might have personally made one of these excuses."

It's so easy to be judgmental when we don't know the whole story. Life can be so much better and sweeter when we start by assuming innocence until we learn more facts. This applies to so many life situations.

Seek first to listen, then be listened to, or seek first to understand, then be understood.

This comes from Stephen R. Covey, in his book, *The 7 Habits of Highly Effective People*. It continues with the theme of listening first before you share your thoughts. Stephen goes into so much more detail about this. If you would like to learn more, check out this book.

Listening is much more important than talking.

Many of us have a strong desire to talk. We want to share what is on our minds. We feel that what we have to say is quite important, from our perspective. That's why we often spend so much time talking and minimal time listening.

Listening, and paying attention to someone else, takes work and concentration. It's easy to get distracted by other things that are happening around us. Even our own thoughts get hijacked by what is being shared. In many cases, it is hijacked about something totally unrelated to the conversation, something that's weighing heavily on our minds.

Listening is more important than talking from many perspectives. We don't learn much if anything, when we're talking. When we listen, we can learn how someone is feeling, what they've done, or how to do something new or in a new way. We benefit from their experiences, maybe directing us toward or away from an activity that was shared, or giving us wisdom about how to engage something differently. Listening is also a tremendously powerful tool in developing and building relationships. Listening might be the best way to convey love.

We were born with one mouth and two ears, and the ears are above the mouth. Maybe there's a reason.

To clarify you understood a message, restate what you heard someone say.

You can provide this valuable service to others by simply saying, "So... (then restate what you thought you've heard)", or, "In summary...", or even, "Let me make sure I understand, I think what I heard was..."

There are many reasons for miscommunication. When I've used this technique, I've been surprised how often I learn that I missed the main point, or maybe even understood the opposite of what was being conveyed. Misunderstanding can be due to: poor articulation of the point by the speaker, a lack of vocabulary or accurate words to convey the point, a miss statement on the part of the messenger; or it could be that the listener only heard part of the message, was distracted, and didn't clearly hear the message, or was dealing with their own baggage on the topic and listened with a strong internal bias that caused them to skew the interpretation of the words they heard.

The goal is to receive the message as it was intended. Restating what you have heard, especially with sensitive topics, is an extremely powerful practice. If you, or the messenger, realize the message wasn't correctly received, this practice provides the opportunity for them to articulate it again in another way, louder, with different or more descriptive words, or maybe just slower.

This technique is one way to ensure better communication. If you don't already use this, give it a try.

Enough talking about me. What do you think about me?

This is a comical way to convey that many of us only want to talk about ourselves. Relationship building is much better when most of the time we are focused on the other person and their activities. Thanks to the late Ed DeCosta for this great reminder. As I typed this point, I just learned he passed away a couple of days ago, at the age of sixty. Ed was a John Maxwell Team faculty member, a great teacher, a mentor, and a friend.

When others are talking, don't write yourself their stories.

I also learned this from Ed DeCosta at a John Maxwell Team live event. I did this all the time. When I heard someone share an experience, I soon cut them off, jumped in, and told them about my similar experience. I would hijack their story. I stole the show from them, cutting them off.

Have you ever done that? It comes quite naturally to many of us. In our own selfish way, we jump to talking about us, leaving them hanging, when they were looking forward to telling us about their experience. This is a terrible way to attempt to build a relationship, it's not listening to them. It's being selfish.

The next time someone starts to tell you about their experience, allow them to stay in their story. Ask a question, or make a statement like, "How interesting. Tell me more." Or, "What was it like? How did it go? When did you do it?" or "Will you do it again?" Let them be the center stage of their conversation, and they will love it, and you, and you will learn, both about them and the experience.

Listen through a person's comments before responding. Wait for a pause, then share your thoughts.

This is a powerful habit. In response to a first, or partial, sentence that's being shared, it's natural to not listen well, but focus, on what we want to say in response. We often jump instantly from focusing on them to us. It's so powerful to use this discipline, to focus on their comments, ensuring they've been able to say all they want to say on a topic. This is so helpful when it comes to building strong relationships, and learning, both more about them and about some aspect of life.

An excellent listener is a valuable friend. Waiting for a pause is one great way to know they've fully made their point and said all they planned to say. For some, this might take a while. They might have a lot on their mind that they would like to share about a topic. When we allow them to do so, we have provided a great relationship environment.

Give this a try and you will see how hard it is to do and how powerful it can be for relationships.

Ask, "What else?" to allow someone to continue to process their thoughts.

Listen through all their thoughts, and potentially ask "What else?" again, if there seems to be more that's deep inside. This is a tip from coaching.

Many of us don't feel heard, known, or understood. When someone else is sharing, rather than jumping in with your thoughts on the topic, try continuing to listen and work to listen beyond the surface, and see what comes. If you're desiring to build a relationship or show love to someone, this is a great investment. We all want to be heard and understood. You can be the one who can help them feel heard, loved, and cared about.

Your listening might even provide them with enough insight to help them address, or solve, their own problem. All you had to do was truly, caringly, and lovingly, listen deeply.

A comment made to you might be more about that person and how they're feeling, than about you and what you said or did.

I'm reflective and introspective. When something bad happens, I usually think first about what I did to possibly cause the problem and what I could have done differently to have prevented it. I think the same way when I interact with others. When another person reacts defensively, or negatively to something I said or did, I think about me and what I did that may have caused that reaction.

I've come to learn that in many cases, what I said, or did, might have been fine, the reaction might be more of a reflection of what is going on within them. They might be frustrated with their current situation or environment. They might be sad, mad, or angry about something else that's happening in their life. I've come to learn that often, it's about them, not me.

This has helped me take some pressure off, helping me feel better about myself when I've likely not been the cause of their reaction.

Communication - Talking

Sticks and stones will break my bones, but words will never hurt me.

I've heard this since grade school. And now I believe it's so wrong. Words are so powerful. A broken bone, or fracture, can be difficult to deal with for days, weeks, or months. But both encouraging and damaging words can stay with us for a lifetime. Words aren't idle. They are empowering and can also be tremendously damaging. Once they are shared, you can't take them back, not fully. Often, the recipient will hang on to those words for years and maybe for the rest of their life. Words can generate feelings, and emotions that can dominate our thoughts, confidence, and actions.

Words are much more powerful than most physical injuries. Keep this in mind as you communicate. Choose your words wisely. They are tremendously powerful.

Tone Is Even More Powerful than Words.

I've shared about the power of our words, both in our head, and verbally, but there is another aspect to communication that can even trump our words. Tone truly sets the stage for any words we say. Good, practical, appropriate words can be quickly turned into accusations, and critical sharp messages simply by the tone we use in conveying them.

It's easy to be blind to the tone that we use when talking to someone, but it is vitally important. To find out how you come across, and what tone you use when you speak, first try to be personally sensitive and aware of how you sound, but more importantly, you may want to ask others about your tone, especially in challenging situations.

You can be right about something, and even use accurate words to convey a message, but your tone will make all the difference in how it is received. Don't underestimate your tone.

Share just a little and only provide more when the listener asks for more.

This one is hard to swallow, but is vital for developing better and deeper relationships, especially with people you don't know well. I can get on a roll and share tiny details when the other person may have no interest. I continually work on this one. But it's true. If someone is truly interested or they are a wonderful listener, they will ask for more when they want it.

Often people can understand our main point without needing to hear all the detail, or content we so deeply want to share. I share this speaking from personal experience, being on both sides. Going into detail about something the other person doesn't care about is a waste of their time and can reflect poorly on us. A great conversationalist says a little and then waits. And they share more only when the listener requests to know more.

This practice can tremendously enhance your communication skills and improve your relationships.

The more you know, the less you need to say.

This is from Jim Rohn. He talks about how little Jesus had to say and how brief so many of his comments were. He didn't need to say a lot due to who He was. The more we become, inside, as a person, the less we have to say to make an impact.

During my corporate career, I noticed that usually the higher the person is in the management or leadership structure, the less they say. It is usually the lowest-level employees who talk the most.

Keep this in mind when you interact with others. Are you the constant talker or are you the wise one who only uses a few words to make your points and share your thoughts? The better and clearer a person's thinking, the fewer words they need to communicate. This is an interesting way to gauge a person's impact on those around them.

Global or general statements are often false and can lead to problems: there are usually exceptions, and they can put others on the defensive.

This one has especially hit home since 2020. There have been so many cases where people speak in global generalities and absolutes.

Absolutes are rarely fully true. When someone uses an absolute statement, the listener often gets defensive, and will in their mind, if not verbally, think or share an example where the statement isn't true.

Global or generalization statements seldom add value but create division. We don't seem to respond well to, "You always... You never....

We can also respond defensively even when a comment isn't made about us. It reduces my respect level when I hear someone regularly using generalized or absolute statements, things like "I can never..., Everyone..., They always..., They all..., and Nothing ever... These statements are loaded with emotion, and they're usually overstated and are weak in facts or content.

It is much better to say something like, "It seems they seldom get my order right, or that road is often crowded and back up, or I often have a hard time getting my phone to..." These are more factual statements that people can relate to without critique, emotion, or defensiveness. These examples share a personal perspective in a limited sense, they don't come across as critical or judgmental about others or all of something.

When possible, it's best to eliminate general statements or absolutes. You will be more factual and better respected by others.

Communicate love in the other person's love language or languages.

This is from the book, *The Five Love Languages*, by Gary Chapman. It's a fantastic book. I won't share the details, but his main point is that we seem to give and receive love based on primarily one or two methods of the five he has identified.

We attempt to communicate love to others in the way we like to receive love. Often that's not the best method to convey love to the other person. You've likely experienced this when you've tried to convey love to someone, and they just don't seem to get it. It seems so clear to us, and for some reason, they just don't get it. It is like trying to say, "I love you." in French when they only understand German. No matter how well, loud, soft, or frequently we try to say it, they don't get it.

If you're interested in learning more, read the book. His five methods are Gifts, Physical Touch, Quality Time, Acts of Service, and Words of Encouragement.

Give it a read and see if a lightbulb goes off for you as well.

Convey your message in the form of a memorable story, that is relatable and powerful, will be retained much longer, and will likely be shared with others.

This comes from the powerful book, *Stories That Stick*, by Kindra Hall. It makes strong points that to help convey our messages it's best to do it through a story or stories. We generally relate better to a story, something that we can imagine, in contrast to just hearing facts, statistics, or points. Through a story, we reach both the mental and the emotional side of our listeners.

We remember storytellers, with their incredible, funny, and surprising examples.

Seek win-win situations.

This is from Stephen R. Covey and *The Seven Habits of Highly Effective People*. With disagreements, he encourages us to focus on finding ways that both sides can win. He encourages us to start by focusing on what both sides have in common, and what both sides want, and then by moving into identifying ways to move forward with those joint goals.

A lot of people think it should be "My way or the highway", only what I want is important. That's an unhealthy way to approach any situation or relationship. If you win with only your perspective and the relationship is destroyed, it isn't much of a win. The goal should be for both parties to win with the things that are most important to each of them, and this can happen much better and more often than you may think. To learn more on this topic, read his book.

Especially with confrontation, first seek common ground, then move to potential options.

This concept was strongly made in the book, *Crucial Conversation*, by Kerry Patterson. One example that was shared was in union negotiations, but the concept applies to any conflict or confrontation. There is almost always common ground between two parties, but the natural focus is on the areas of difference.

By focusing first on the areas of common ground it's much easier to realize that the two parties aren't as far apart as they may have thought. By building on common elements, it's much easier to come to practical solutions that can be beneficial to both parties.

This works. I've used it many times. Work to find the things you agree on, before trying to address your areas of difference.

Before sharing something challenging, ask for permission. There isn't much value in sharing something when the other person isn't open to hearing it.

Sharing something with someone who is not interested in your content, or recommendation, seldom results in any real benefit, and can even create a negative impact if they perceive we are pushing something that they're not interested in.

By asking if they would like to hear your comment on a particular topic, you can immediately learn if they feel it might be helpful. At a minimum, if they say, "Yes", you're likely going to share your comment with someone who will be more open-minded. There is a much better chance that your comment could have a positive impact.

It is those of us who push our criticism, or solutions on other people, who seldom see the results we hope for. And it's a shame to put a relationship at risk by pushing our agenda.

If the response is "No", generally it's best to hold off sharing your comments. Only if you're in a conversation that's critical to their health or is an immediate life or death threat for them, or someone they might harm, then, because it's so important, it's worth sharing your comments with the potential of damaging the relationship.

Give this a try.

Don't say "Good job" but rather speak how pleased, happy, and proud someone must be themselves because they produced a specific result.

This gem came from a parent training session at church, the session was called, *The Parent Toolkit Workshop*. It provided several helpful tips and suggestions for us as young parents and many of the concepts also applied to communication with adults.

When it comes to praise, we should share specifics, and say it in a way the person can easily understand what they did well, directing the attention away from us being the one providing the feedback. The goal is for them to know and see the good in their own performance and results. We should encourage them on the specific things they did well.

In contrast, the instructor shared how limited the value of a compliment is when it's general and comes from a person in authority. It is of value, but nowhere near as helpful for future performance as it could be.

She shared a good example of something like this.

Johnny, you must be so proud of how well you spelled each word, stayed in the lines, put a period at the end of each sentence, and used a noun and a verb.

By providing this level of detail, Johnny didn't just know he did something well, but also why, and what made it good, so he could know what to do in the future to continue his excellent performance.

This simple example for a child was easy to understand, but could also be used with adults, direct reports, or friends who are helping us. Like,

Thanks for your help with compiling the report, your timeliness was quite helpful for my speech, and the way you laid it out, using the graph on the horizontal page made it easy to see the point. You sure know how to add value to a project. Thanks.

This approach and these few extra words can be extremely helpful when it comes to their future performance. General compliments are helpful but don't provide anywhere near the same long-term value.

Some people, if they don't know, you can't tell them.

I don't remember where I heard this one, but I get a chuckle from it each time I think of it. It's so true. It says, "Some people", but I think it's most of us. There seem to be so many blind spots within each of us, and if we're not already aware of them, we just don't seem to be able to see them, even when someone directly tries to communicate them to us. What they're sharing just doesn't make sense to us.

After hearing this quote, I immediately had people and situations come to mind, people I had tried to help with a topic who were nowhere near able to see it in their own lives. Also, there are people I knew it wouldn't be worth confronting. They wouldn't accept the feedback and would get defensive, damaging our relationship, or it was too small of a matter and was not worth addressing.

It's great to be able to see this in others, but it is even more helpful to assume that I'm likely the same. Unless I work hard at it, I will also be closed and not see the blind spot someone might be trying to share with me. I hope I'm more aware and open than some others, but I'm sure I still have blind spots that others still just don't seem to be able to convey to me.

How about you? Are you open to comments about you that you might not easily see in yourself? It's valuable feedback.

There is only one way to get anybody to do anything, by making the person want to do it.

This comes from Dale Carnegie from, *How to Make Friends and Influence People*. At my first reading of this, this seemed like a radical thought, but in the end, I believe it's true. People do things because they want to do them. They perceive there is some benefit to them in the short or long term.

The best way to get someone to do something is to take the time to think through reasons they could want to do it. When you put enough time and effort into that, you can usually find a way, or reason, they could want to perform a task, and if not, you can change the structure of the request so it will give them some benefit in the long run.

Keep this one in mind when you work with others or are hoping for their assistance.

When asking a person for something, focus on "what they want" (WTW). There is usually a good reason they could want to do what you are asking.

This is the same concept, shared in Dale Carnegie's book, *How to Win Friends and Influence People*. I shortened my reference to the concept to be, WTW. I use it as a prompt to think about why someone could want to do what I'm asking them to do, versus, just focusing on me and what I need for them to do. I can usually come up with a beneficial reason for the other person to want to do what I'm asking of them.

An example could be me wanting someone to provide constructive feedback on something I've written. My motive may be to get help, but they can also benefit as well. Rather than just asking, can you review this and provide me with some feedback? I could say, "Since you love ninja so much, and you enjoy learning more about it, would you be willing to give me feedback on my ninja document? And I would be glad to consider including many of your personal suggestions into the content, I will credit you as a reviewer of the material, and I will also provide you with a free copy of the final published version. Would you be interested in helping? In this way, I've provided many potential reasons why this person could want to take the time to read and provide me with feedback.

This concept can apply to practically anything we ask of someone. And it works well when we're willing to take the time to think about them and what could benefit them. This concept has worked well in so many cases. It can be beneficial to them, and me, as it becomes a partnership relationship rather than a one-way transaction request.

Leadership

Manage things and lead people, not the other way around.

Author Stephen R. Covey conveyed this concept. He made the point that many people try to manage people, inside a tight box, and his belief is we should lead people, and help them to become all they can be with our leadership support, not share with them every detail of how we want something to be completed.

He believes it's appropriate to manage things that don't have minds, but that we should lead people, letting those we work with, or who work for us, use their hearts and minds to be engaged and creative with their actions.

Chapter 11:

Employment

We get paid for bringing value to the marketplace. It takes time to bring value to the marketplace, but we get paid for the value, not the time.

This is another Jim Rohn gem. It is so easy to think we get paid for time, the time we are at work. But in the big picture, we're really paid for value, which is why some people make a lot more money than others. Two people might work the same number of hours, but their pay rates can be significantly different, one makes $15 an hour and another person makes $25 or even $55 an hour, or more. It isn't just because they work more hours, it's that they provide more value to their company or to a customer.

And as Jim states, it takes time to develop ourselves so that we can provide more value. We need time to learn and develop new skills, to become more valuable to others. This can include skills in communication, technology, physical abilities, and deeper and better thinking.

We get paid for the value we bring to others. Focus on that, not the hours you work.

This change in focus provided tremendous benefit to me with my career.

The most important question to ask on the job isn't "What am I getting?" but rather, "What am I becoming?"

This line from Jim Rohn caused a major shift in my thinking. I had always looked at a job from a "getting" perspective. What am I being paid? What are the benefits? What are the opportunities? What about me? That's a normal way to look at a job, right? No. Jim's comment resonated and made sense when I was promoted to the senior program manager level at work. After serving in that role for a period I was asked about my interest in moving up to the next level of leadership within the organization. This concept totally changed my perspective. I no longer saw this as an opportunity to gain more power, more money, larger bonuses, and more perks.

I now looked at it from the perspective of who I would become if I worked closely with the people who were currently at that level, and... I wanted to have nothing to do with becoming like them. There were about 12 members at the next level, and I simply didn't want to take on their perspectives, priorities, attitudes, and management styles. I was reading many leadership books at that time, and I wanted to lead in the new ways I was learning, not from a dictatorial, intimidation perspective, like so many of them were demonstrating to our team. I promptly turned down the opportunity to move up in the organization, based on who I would likely become if I took on a role like that, with them.

If it was a smaller team, I might have had an interest in trying to influence them in what I believed to be better leadership practices, but there were too many of them and they were already quite ingrained in their styles and attitudes. I had already been rebuked for trying to lead people rather than manage their every move and action. I wanted nothing to do with the "My way or the highway" approach to what they called leadership.

We're significantly influenced by the people and environments we're exposed to. If you don't already think this way, I encourage you to start asking the question, "What am I becoming when I participate in this environment? If it won't help you become who you want to be, it's time to make a change. Others rub off on us, both the good and bad. Make sure you live and work within the type of influences you want to be around.

My father taught me to always do more than you get paid for, as an investment in your future.

This is from Jim Rohn. The message was basically, do more than you're paid for, creating more value for your employer, making yourself so valuable that they can't afford to lose you, so they must reward you financially, and likely want to promote you. This is a version of paying it forward, and over the years it has resulted in tremendous financial rewards for me.

This contrasts with some of my direct reports who had complained that they hadn't been paid enough for what they were already doing. It was interesting to watch how their careers halted, went to a standstill, and in some cases, even went backwards.

Opportunities continued to come my way, with financial rewards that followed, nice financial rewards. I wasn't in a standard career path role, where there were logical next steps or promotions, but opportunities continued to come my way. I started as a media communication manager. My wife described my career as being like an octopus. I started as a company video producer, then they asked if I could also produce the monthly company print news magazine. I said, "Yes." Then they asked if I could also manage the self-development book and audio tape library system for the company. Again, I said, "Yes." Then they asked if I could lead the company's annual all-manager meeting, and I said, "Yes." Then they asked if I could help provide some management and leadership training, and again, my answer was, "Yes." Next, I joined our recruiters on college campuses, helping recruit young new Executive Training Program candidates. Then I was asked to take on managing our Human Resources division budget and I said, "Yes." This all happened while I continued to be the video producer and media communication manager for the company. There were several other roles I took on and then I was asked if I would be willing to move into the company Compensation Manager position, helping determine and manage the pay rates for all employees in the company. I said, "Yes." The opportunities continued. I was swallowing up roles like an octopus, with all its tentacles, continually reaching out and taking on more roles. I never asked for a raise, and I received many, and some were quite large.

It pays to provide more than you're currently paid to do. Give it a try. Stay with it. People, managers, and leaders see value, and highly value people who deliver it.

Chapter 12:

Money

Money Management

Formal education will make you a living; self-education will make you a fortune.

This is a gem from Jim Rohn. He has a lot of financial insights. He challenges us to work hard on educating ourselves, beyond what we gain from formal schooling. Formal education is beneficial, in high school, college, or technical schools, but our greatest value comes from continuing to learn about topics, like ourselves, others, life, business, communication, leadership, management, time management, planning, and sales. Continuing to learn about these and other things will make you a more valuable person and employee.

Self-education is so powerful.

Live like nobody else so that later you can live like nobody else.

This is from financial guru Dave Ramsey. I love this line.

For years my wife and I had been making a lot of hard or tough financial decisions and I was feeling like I was living like nobody else in my circles. It felt like my peers wore nicer clothes, drove nicer and more expensive cars, had much nicer and larger houses, had special memberships, and ate at many expensive restaurants that I didn't. And it was true. I didn't have many of these things for years. I was living like nobody else.

Then came age 56. We began to live like nobody else in a much different way. We were blessed and had made a lot of consistent hard decisions for many years and we were then able to live with financial freedom. Living only on our investments, not from me having to go to work each day. And unlike many of my peers, who were still working, grinding away, day after day, for many more years, I was living with financial freedom.

When I retired, I was provided with a severance package which provided us with freedom a year earlier than I had planned, but our long-term plan had paid off, it worked. We were now living like nobody else, at least not like most of the population. I was able to retire ten years earlier than almost all my peers.

Since retiring we have had the freedom to invest our time the way we want without having to work a daily job. Dave was right, "Live like nobody else so that later you can live like nobody else." Our freedom came at a pretty young age, but could have been even earlier had I learned many of the concepts in *Gems* earlier in life. I've enjoyed living with this freedom for over 11 years, and if I live into my 90s, I might have another 25 or more years to enjoy it.

I wish the same freedom for you. I urge you to make the important tough financial decisions early in life so you can have the same type of freedom later.

A - B = C: Spend less than you make. Solve for a positive C.

This point has been drilled into me for a long time, probably from my parents, who lived on a budget. We must live on less money than we make, not more than we make. I was also raised to give 10% of my income to the church or charities. I've done that, and more, all my life.

I've also come to believe I should pay myself, putting money away for the future, saving and investing, rather than overspending and supporting a lavish lifestyle.

I also learned from the book, *The Millionaire Next Door*, that many of the millionaires of the past 50 years are those who simply lived on less money than they made. It is the ones who spend and look like, "Millionaires" who often spend more than they make, live in fear of collapse, and have little money to their name. They spend their money before they even earn it.

Living by this one simple concept, A – B = C, will provide you with so much safety, peace, and confidence in your life. It requires making a lot of hard choices, but it's so worth it, especially in the long run.

Tell your money where to go and know where it went. Establish and live on a budget.

I think I first heard this concept from Jim Rohn, "Tell your money where to go, don't just let it go anywhere it wants at any time it wants." This is another way of saying, establish a budget.

Identify how much money you have coming in and tell it where to go, based on your priorities. Decide how much you want to give to those less fortunate, pay yourself early by putting some money into savings and investments, then pay down debt if you have it, and finally, allocate what you can afford to live on for housing, food, clothes, entertainment, and so on.

Decide in advance how much money will go to what, before you make the money. These decisions can be tough, especially when you first start to live on a budget, but as the years pass and your income grows, it gets easier and easier to fund more money on the things you want to do, not just the things you need to do.

I've lived on a budget since leaving home, at age 18, that's nearly 50 years. It can be done, and it works. I also tracked my spending to ensure I lived within my budget. It's not easy, but it absolutely works. This is critical to getting yourself into a healthy financial position, and setting yourself up for living in financial freedom. This has truly been one of the most basic and important elements that has allowed me to move into financial freedom in my mid-50s.

Tell your money where to go. Be its boss. Don't let it go wherever it wants. It will radically improve your future.

Owe no man anything, but to love one another: for he that loveth another hath fulfilled the law.

This is a simple message from Romans 13:8 in the Bible, stating we're not to owe others money, service, not anything. Just love them. I'm convinced this is a great principle.

When it comes to buying a house, getting an education, or buying a car we might need to borrow money for a time, but the goal should always be to pay them off as soon as practical, hopefully way ahead of any repayment plan.

It's a great feeling to owe no man anything. We were able to be in this position at age 52. We finally paid off our home, which was our last debt. Then all our income was allocated to additional savings and giving and toward our general living expenses. I was no longer paying interest to anyone for the money I'd borrowed. This is a tremendous feeling, an extremely freeing place to be. If we were to lose income or experience a catastrophic event, we would be able to use all our money to recover. Our money is no longer going toward paying for a place to live or for cars to get around.

Make it your goal to owe no man anything, especially not credit card companies that charge very high interest rates.

Plan and execute toward financial freedom, which is attainable in the United States, if you're intentional.

This is from Jim Rohn.

With the freedom we have in the United States, if we start early, have the right perspective, the right knowledge, and consistent discipline, financial freedom, not having to work at a day job to live well, is possible for many of us, and well prior to retirement age. And even if we don't achieve full financial freedom, we can be in much better financial shape when it's time to retire. Jim believed it and lived it, and so have I, as I mentioned, retiring ten years earlier than the typical retirement age.

When I retired after 33 years of hard work in the corporate world, I realized that if I lived till age 90, or later, I could live with financial freedom for more than 33 years, which would be my life act number two, a much freer period, less stressful, more creative, with broader experiences, and with much more family time.

You can also live by these principles. They are within your control, your grasp, your power. Take them seriously.

Penny wise and pound foolish

This is a general statement I've heard much of my life. I believe there is a lot of wisdom in it.

I've known people who spent so much time counting their pennies, their tiny purchases but had no idea how they were doing financially on the grand scale. They buy cheap things that wear out and break easily, and spend less money whenever they can, not thinking from a long-term perspective.

I believe it's extremely wise to make financial decisions based on a long-term perspective. You can often get even better deals by making longer-term purchases that might cost more on the front end but pay off well in the long run.

Sometimes, it's better to trash something that's broken and doesn't work well, rather than continue to spend money trying to fix it. Sometimes it's easy to be so focused on spending money to fix something, and the better choice is to see the big picture and realize that you don't even use or need that item any longer. It's no longer serving you well.

Do your best to make wise long-term decisions, even if it initially costs more.

Focus on your net worth.

Focus on increasing what you own and reducing and eliminating what you owe. Invest in things that grow in value.

Net Worth is a fancy financial term, but it basically means what you're worth, financially, when you add up all you own, and all you owe, the result is your net worth.

This is a simple example. If you have $300 in your savings account and a bike worth $60 and then also you owe your sister $50, your net worth is $310, $300+$60-$50=$310.

When you use this simple formula, you can quickly and easily determine your net worth, how much financial value you have. You could say this number reflects how well you've managed the money you've made during your life.

If you've been working for three years and made $30,000 a year, you've made or earned $90,000. The question is, what have you done with the $90,000? How much of it do you have left for your security, your future, and your long-term financial freedom?

I've focused on my net worth for many years. My goal was to continually increase it to the point where I had enough to live on without having to work. That's called financial freedom. That's what I was working toward.

I think most of us would like to be in that position, to be our own boss and to get to use our time the way we want. That's what financial freedom brings.

What is your net worth? I encourage you to learn your net worth now, be it small, large, or even negative. Your goal should be to try and make that number more positive, growing each month, one month at a time. In time, it will dramatically improve your life and future.

What is your debt-to-asset ratio?

This is another very interesting way to look at your money. It relates to the net worth concept I just shared but in a different way.

Your asset-to-debt ratio works this way. If you have $7,000 of assets, things of value, clothes, car, bike, and other things, and you owe $3,500 on your car, your debt-to-asset ratio is 50%. Half of what you own is fully yours and the other half you would have to sell if you had to pay off your debt.

The goal is to get the ratio down to 0%, so you have no debt, but that takes time. In the interim, your goal should be to reduce that hypothetical 50% ratio to a smaller number. Maybe in two months, you could get it down to 47%, and then down even more in a couple more months.

You can reduce this number by paying off your monthly car payment, and maybe even by paying more on the payment. You could also increase the amount you save each month, to increase your total assets, the things you own.

If you work overtime, receive a special bonus, or get some type of raise, or a tax refund, you could reduce this ratio even more by paying off even more debt or increasing your savings and investments. Each little bit counts. Make it a game and see if you can reduce your debt-to-asset ratio by two points every three months. Keep it moving in the right direction till you get to the point where you've finally achieved 0%. Then you can truly celebrate, all your money that was paying off your debt is now yours to… tell it where to go… to reallocate wherever you want, hopefully, some of it to even more monthly savings and investments. Some of it can also be allocated to increasing your lifestyle, more travel, eating out, new clothes, or whatever you believe is most important. That's a day to celebrate.

Pay off all your debt, starting with the smallest chunk, regardless of the interest rate.

This came from Dave Ramsey. It seems to be a wise strategy.

If you find yourself in debt to multiple businesses, make the minimum monthly payment on each loan, and then work at aggressively paying off the smallest one first, even if it has a lower interest rate. When possible, work hard to pay more each month, paying the debt off ahead of schedule. If the minimum payment is $200 a month, find a way to pay off $225 or $250 each month, shortening the time you will remain in debt for that loan.

There is a tremendous emotional high each time we pay off a debt, and especially when we can pay off all of it. We are emotional beings. We need to acknowledge and celebrate our emotional reaction to each of these exciting debt-freeing milestones.

Once that first loan or debt is paid off, the goal is to apply that same payment money towards the next smallest debt, doing this repeatedly until all your debt is paid off. Keep applying those payments to the next smallest loan, working to get it paid off. Do this until you are debt-free, and then you can apply even more money to your savings and investments for your long-term future.

Remember, each time you make a payment on any debt, you're increasing your net worth, and your financial value. That's exciting. You're moving closer to financial freedom.

Supply and Demand

This concept seems to reflect the way things work in our society. It's the law of economics. If you have something that no one wants, it's difficult to get people to pay for it, it's worthless and soon disappears, it ceases to exist, and ceases to be built, provided, and available. People no longer wanted an eight-track player, when cassette tapes were introduced, and then CDs and DVDs, replaced them. There was no more demand for those older products, they had been replaced by something else that people wanted.

When many people want something, we call that, "Demand." In those situations, many people or companies build a product or service and provide it for a cost. The more people that want it and the less it's available to the public, the more it will cost the customer. This is a simple rule followed by entrepreneurs and companies; they find something that they can produce or provide, a product or service, and provide it to the masses, this is called, "supply". When this happens, it results in businesses making a lot of money.

If only a few sources can provide a product or service, the supply is limited, which also increases the price. Even if the demand is high, if there is a lot of availability of the product or service, the price will be lower.

The goal is to find the sweet spot, where demand is high, and the supply is low. One of the challenges is that demand continually changes. At one point, everybody wants a certain type of tablet or phone, until someone else provides better features and the demand moves to that new product or service.

Understanding this concept helps us understand how the world around us works. And if you have some entrepreneurial tendencies, to be successful, this is the way you need to think, you need to always be looking for ways to see the demand that exists today or will exist in the future, and then provide that product or service that will meet that demand.

Investments

Put more of your money into investments than into savings.

Jim Rohn encourages us to save some of our money, not spend it all, saving for our future. But he also believes it is even better to invest our money rather than saving it.

If you just save money at home, it remains safe, but it is stagnant, it isn't working for you. If you put money in a bank savings or checking account, you make some money, usually at a small, fixed percentage, which is better than nothing, but is nowhere near as beneficial as investing it in companies, where they work with your money, for you.

With investing, the risk is higher than with putting your money in a bank checking or savings account, but the potential rewards are so much higher. It's appropriate to have a mix, some money in a bank savings or checking account, to help cover your expenses in the short term, three-to six months. But you should also have a significant amount invested in strong companies that you believe in.

The difference between the two options can be dramatic. A simple example would be that if you put $500 in a savings account and you made 1% interest a year, at the end of the year you would have made $5. If you had invested that money in a strong company and earned 6% that year, you would have made $30. Staying with the same analogy, if you had $5,000 in savings, you would have made $50, and had you invested it, you would have made $300.

I would recommend investing in businesses over the savings account, and as I stated above, I would encourage you to have a mix, a portion in savings and a lot more in investments, especially if you're young and have a lot of time for your money to work for you.

Put some, and hopefully a lot of your saved money into investments, and over time you can reap many benefits. There is more risk with investments, but based on history, even when you lose money, or it remains stagnant for a period, over time it will recover.

My experience since my retirement has been getting an average of between six and even 16% a year return on our money, which is way better than the example I provided above.

If you had $100,000, a 16% return would mean you would have made $16,000, just by letting companies work with your money for the year. You're doing nothing but investing, just waiting, and letting time pass. What an awesome way to live.

Can you imagine how much you would make if over time you had $500,000 or a million dollars in those types of investments? You would have made between $60,000 and $160,000 for the year. Wow!

Invest a significant portion of your savings. It can provide incredible benefits for you and move you closer to true financial freedom. It has for us.

The rich invest their money and spend what is left; the poor spend their money and invest what is left.

Again, this is from Jim Rohn. This boils down to priorities. Invest first, then figure out what you have left to live on and find a way to make it work.

If you spend your money first, you will likely not have any money left to invest in your future. You're hanging yourself and your future if you live only for today.

You don't have to start with much money, it can be as low as $25, $50, or $75 a month, going into savings, or even better, into an investment. But you need to pay yourself first, right off the bat, and invest in your future each time you receive your paycheck. Over time, when you receive pay increases, increase what you invest for your future, and then raise your standard of living, in that order.

That's how the rich live. This shift in prioritization can make a world of difference for you.

Start investing early, at least a little, toward your long-term financial freedom.

Money growth takes time. The earlier you start, the better it will be for you. It will continue to grow if you keep it invested. You just need to be consistent and patient.

If you start by setting aside $50 a month toward savings, you can save over $600 within one year. If you invest your money and it grows an average of 5% a year, that $600 could grow to $630 during the first year.

When you get to the place where your additional monthly savings grow to $1,000, the 5% growth becomes another $50, your money grows to $1,050.

It's exciting to watch it grow over the years, as you continue to save and invest more money. As your money grows to $5,000, a 5% growth becomes another $250, and $10,000 becomes $500 of additional money, and $25,000 can result in another $1,250 of investment growth.

Think about the possibilities of your future when you continue to save and invest more money. If you get to the $100,000 investment mark, just by letting your money work for you during a year, at a 5% growth rate, you would make another $5,000, doing nothing on your own.

This can continue as long as you continue to save and invest. At $500,000 of investment and a 5% growth rate, your money could grow by $25,000 a year, just by being invested in strong companies, as they work with your money. They use your money to make a profit for themselves, and then they share that profit with you.

Imagine if your investments were to grow to $1,000,000 (one million dollars), at that point, a 5% growth rate results in an additional $50,000 for the year.

Once you get to the place where your investment growth rate covers all your expenses for a year, you've achieved the point of financial freedom. You no longer need to work each day to make money, you have what you need to live.

Let's get creative. If your money grew to $2,000,000 (two million dollars), at a 5% return you could make $100,000 a year, just through your investments. Of course, all of this takes time, years, and consistency with saving and investing.

You may have some years that provide less than a 5% rate of growth, and at times, even the loss of some of your money. But in my experience, the average growth rate over the years has been much higher than 5%, as much as triple that number during some periods, over a 15% growth rate. Imagine that.

Start as early as you can, now, regardless of your age.

"Compound interest is the eighth wonder of the world. He who understands it, earns it. He who doesn't, pays it." Compounding Works.

This is a quote attributed to Albert Einstein. It's another way to convey the message I just shared. When you get interest paid to you on your money, then you have more money to earn interest on for the next year, it continues to grow on top of itself if you keep it invested in a bank or with a company that pays you interest.

In simple terms, $1,000 at a 2% interest rate becomes $1,020. The next year that same money will grow to $1,040 and by the third year, building on that $1,040, your money will grow to $1,061. And it will continue to grow year after year when you keep investing it somewhere that pays you interest on your money. It works.

I agree that it's a "wonder of the world" and many don't use this tool and it costs them severely. People who don't save money or invest it, often borrow money from the bank to live, they're the ones who pay interest to the bank on the money they've borrowed. This is what allows a bank to pay interest to those of us who have invested our money with a bank.

Don't be a borrower, be a saver and investor. It can create a wonderful future for you.

Invest half of all your raises or bonuses in long-term investments, so they can go to work for you.

I love this tip from Jim Rohn. You might not have much to save or invest when you first start this valuable practice, but once an income increase comes along, through a raise, salary increase, bonus, inheritance, or any other additional income, you have tremendous new power.

Jim encourages us to save or invest half of the additional money. You were able to live off your prior income, so why not use half to invest in your future, by increasing your savings and investments and limiting how much you increase your lifestyle, use the other half of the new money there.

A bank can help you learn ways to invest your money. When you do this year after year, it can really add up. If you start by saving $50 a month and then the next year, invest half of your income increase, maybe another $50, raising it to $100 a month. After five years it could grow to $300 a month, or $3,600 a year, and after 10 years you could increase your new investment to $550 a month, or $6,600 a year. At 20 years you could be saving and investing over $1,000 a month, or over $12,000 a year toward your future. All this can happen just by intentionally putting half of your raises and bonuses to work for you by investing it.

I won't go through the detailed math, but if you received a 5% return on your money each of those years, you could have created an investment portfolio for yourself of over $175,000, all by making small, continual, increases to your investment portfolio over a 20-year period, all from your raises or bonuses. This was a conservative estimate. It could be significantly more if you increase your savings by more than $50 a month each year.

This is an amazing process that works if you do it. Put your money to work for you and your future.

Profits are better than wages. Wages make you a living; profits can make you a fortune.

I grew up focused on working hours to get paid by my employer for the hours I worked. This is an interesting twist from Jim Rohn.

Wages are the money you make by working "for" someone. With wages, you're dependent on someone else to pay you a negotiated rate, usually for an hour of service that you have provided. Increases come on occasion, maybe annually for some people, and they're often anywhere from 1-5%. By working hard and consistently providing great service to your employer you can increase your pay rate over time.

Some also work for a salary, a designated amount of money for taking on and executing certain responsibilities. An example would be getting paid $36,000 a year, or $3,000 a month for managing a store, or department. Your hours aren't tracked. It is assumed you will work a minimum of 40 hours a week, and likely many more to get your work completed. You are not paid by the hour, but rather by the amount of work you have committed to do. You are still being paid by an employer, and depending on how well you complete your work, you can also receive raises for either performing well or taking on additional responsibilities. I was paid a salary during my 33-year professional working career. These are two ways that many people are paid at their jobs, at an hourly rate or through a salary.

In contrast, a profit is the incremental money that you make, beyond the cost of producing and delivering a product or a service. This is what companies earn by providing a product or service for their customers. As an employee, they pay you from their revenue and profit. When you produce a product or service generating a profit, your profit is dependent on how much your products or services are in demand, and how much customers are willing to pay for them. The more people who want to buy them, the more you can charge, and the greater your profit.

With wages, you're paid primarily for your time, whereas with profits you're paid for your product or service.

Wages are usually at a fixed rate, and the number of hours we can work in a week is limited, maybe 40. Some people for short periods might work up to 80 hours a week, but that's extremely exhausting and not normally sustainable. With wages, if you earn $15 an hour, and work a 40-hour week, for four weeks, or 160 hours, you would make $2,400 for the month.

With profits, if you can produce a product or service, and sell it for $3 more than it costs to produce it and deliver it (say it costs $20 to make and you can sell it for $23), and you sell 500 of them for the month, your profit would be $1,500. If you could sell 2,000 of them a month, which would be a 500-a-week rate, you would make $3,000 for the month. If you provide an excellent product or service, and a lot of people want it, you could raise your price to charge $5 more than it costs to produce and deliver it. If you were able to do that and you sold 3,000 of these high-demand products over the month, you would make $15,000 for the month.

Profit depends on your ability to produce a great product or service that's highly desired by customers. You can do this yourself, or partner with others, or you can invest your money with an established business that you believe in, that does the same thing, and let them generate a product or deliver a service and make a profit and have them share some of their profit with you.

Profits are truly better than wages when you can generate them.

Are you paying other people to make money or a profit for you?

Maybe another way to look at this would be to ask, metaphorically, "Have you hired others to work for you, generating a profit for you?" You're in essence paying other people to work for you when you invest money in a company. You're basically buying what is called company stock. You become a part owner of their business, and all you do is pay money to them to buy a part of their business. They do the rest of the work. They use your money to run their business and make money.

They either pay you interest on the money you invested, usually a percent of your money, or they pay you dividends, which is sharing some of the profit that they've made recently. And their (and your) value can increase when the company value increases, resulting in your portion of the company being worth more money.

When you spend your money or keep it in a drawer at home, no one is working for you. The money is either gone or sitting around doing nothing. When you save the money in a bank or invest it in a company, you're putting it to work as other people work for you. You are just letting time pass as you do other things, whether it's working a job to make more money and investing it, or you might be financially free and be spending your time doing the things that you love or feel are important, while others work for you making more money for you.

Don't waste your money that you worked so hard to earn. Make it work for you by investing in it, creating for you a more financially free future.

Buy a cow, pay someone to raise it, buy another one, from the milk produced and sold, then continue the process.

This is another tremendous analogy. Investing in a business to make money is like saving some money and then buying a cow. Then feeding it, having it produce milk, and then selling the milk to make more money. First, you buy more food for the cow and then you save the rest of the money so you can buy another cow to produce more milk. Then you hire someone to take care of and milk the two cows and repeat the process till you have many cows that produce a lot of milk to sell.

Once you get to the point where you make enough money from the milk you sell, you can stop working your day job. You have enough money to live on from all your cows and the milk they produce for you that you can sell.

You could do the same with other product-producing animals like chickens, or with land and crops, houses, apartment buildings, and many other money-producing avenues, it doesn't have to be cows.

This is what it's like when you invest your money with a business, they work hard to produce something, a product, or a service, that they sell to others, producing a profit for the company and for you.

This is such a great analogy. Go buy a cow, or invest your money in a business you believe in. Have them go to work for you.

Create multiple streams of income to provide yourself with more safety and less risk.

When we have multiple sources of something, we face less risk of loss. If we have multiple stores available where we can buy food, we have reduced the risk of running out of it. If we have just one store, then there is a chance that at times, it might run out of the type of food we want.

The same is true for your income or pay. This is one of the reasons that having your own business can be more desirable. When you work for one company, you're dependent on that company to continue to provide employment for you. If they release you or fire you, you're without income.

If you work for multiple companies, or better yet, produce or provide something to multiple customers, then your risk of losing all your income is much lower. You might lose a few customers, but not all of them, and likely you might also be gaining additional customers at the same time.

Although this may seem riskier, if you can provide a quality service or product at a market-fair price, then in some ways, there is less risk to you than being dependent on one customer or company.

Another alternative is to generate income through multiple activities at the same time. An example of this would be to produce and sell some product, paintings, photographs, a tool, or a decoration; and at the same time also get paid for public speaking; then also be a consultant to companies that need and want your expertise; and produce and provide a product people can buy on-line, like a book or newsletter; and also have some financial investments in other companies. When you do many of these types of things, part-time, and have multiple types of income on an ongoing basis, you have less financial risk.

The possibilities are limitless. Make some wise investment decisions and you can improve your future dramatically.

Conclusion

The progression of life is like building a brick wall, you must first establish the foundation and then you can continue to build upon it with additional bricks. These core thoughts were tremendously powerful foundational bricks for me, over the years many additional bricks have been added on top of each of these. The earlier you learn key life concepts the more time you can build upon them, time to improve, enhance, and perfect them, significantly benefiting your life and the lives of those around you.

Over the years I've grown and changed a lot. And many people have helped influence my life. By reading *Gems* you've seen how people like Jim Rohn, John Maxwell, Maxwell Maltz, Brian Tracy, Stephen R. Covey, Darren Hardy, and my parents have helped positively shape me. I'm so thankful that I took the time to read and listen to them. They have made a world of difference in my life.

I've shared a lot of quotes and concepts. I hope you're not overwhelmed, but rather stimulated and encouraged. There's a lot you can do to create a better future that's within your control. Go back and review the points of *Gems*, maybe a quote a day, or section a week. Read it many times to continue to gain more value from it. The best investment is in yourself. Invest in You.

Share with others the concepts that have been most helpful to you. Give them the gift of new ideas. And you can share your copy of *Gems*, or even better, give a copy as a gift, for a graduation, birthday, key life milestone, or celebration. Share your new wealth of knowledge and wisdom. Don't keep it to yourself.

I hope you have an incredible future, much better than you've ever dreamed. I'm convinced you can. Go make it happen.

Bonuses

Seven Recommended Leaders and Authors

- James Allen
- Darren Hardy
- Maxwell Maltz
- John Maxwell
- Jim Rohn
- Brian Tracy
- John Wooden

Eight Recommended Books or CDs

- 15 Indisputable Laws of Growth – John Maxwell
- As A Man Thinketh – James Allen
- The Bible
- Change Your Thinking, Change Your Life – Brian Tracy
- The Compound Effect – Darren Hardy
- Psycho Cybernetics – Maxwell Maltz
- Today Matters – John Maxwell
- The Weekend Seminar – Jim Rohn (CD)

More about Well Done Life Services

Contact Information

Cell phone: 614.787.8591 (call or text)

Email: chriswarnky@gmail.com

Facebook: welldonelife

Website: welldone-life.com

Blog: http://cwarnky.wordpress.com

Well Done Life Series Books

Chris has written a number of books concerning how to live a better life, including *How to Refocus Your Life, The Coach Approach,* and *Turning Gray.*

Heart of a Ninja Series Books

Chris has also written six *Heart of a Ninja Series* books, including *The Heart of a Ninja: Stretch Your Boundaries!*

Acknowledgments

I'm thankful to our awesome Creator/God for providing me with peace and many great relationships and experiences during my first 67 years of life.

Thanks, Carolyn, for your love and support. I can't imagine going through anything without you, to walk through life's successes, failures, and disappointments. I love you.

Thanks for your love and support Mom and Dad, Tim (our son) and Bonnie, and Michelle (our daughter) and Joel.

About the Author

Chris Warnky is 67 and has been married to Carolyn May Warnky for over 45 years. He has two adult children: his son Tim who lives in Cleveland, Ohio with his wife Bonnie, with their two daughters Hannah and Lydia; and his daughter Michelle who lives in Willard, Ohio with her husband Joel and their daughter, Grace. He maintains good relationships with his children, immediate and extended family, and friends and coworkers.

He's the author of ten books, including *How to Refocus Your Life*, *The Coach Approach*, and *Turning Gray*, and six books about his ninja warrior experience.

Chris was a professional executive and life coach, and a thought-provoking speaker through his business, Well Done Life. He is a certified coach, speaker, and trainer with the John Maxwell Team. He served two years on the organization's President's Advisory Council. He served two  terms as president of the International Coach Federation Columbus Charter Chapter. He also achieved the Toastmasters International "Competent Communicator" designation.

Chris has over three decades of corporate leadership experience, including 20 years as a vice president at Bank One/JP Morgan Chase.

He served in leadership roles with Linworth Road Church, Upward Youth Basketball, Westerville Christian Community Church, the International Television Association, and Grace Community Chapel.

Chris has read about and applied concepts from over 500 books on coaching, leadership (both self and team), team building, productivity, effectiveness, communication, marriage, family, and budgeting.

He was debt-free by the age of 52, retired from corporate employment at age 56, and has traveled to over 25 countries across the world, with more to come.

Chris is an active, training ninja warrior. He competed in the 2017 *American Ninja Warrior Cleveland City Qualifier* and has competed in numerous ninja competitions. He's also an MLAB OH Ninja Lite instructor and offers personal one-on-one ninja-lite-level training sessions.

He has been a Christian for over 55 years. His relationship with God is the basis for everything he does.

www.ingramcontent.com/pod-product-compliance
Lightning Source LLC
LaVergne TN
LVHW051952060526
838201LV00059B/3613